I0531093

MINDEFUSEMENT

Ronald Huereca

MediaRon LLC

Mindefusement

ISBN: 978-0-578-46985-0

BOOK DESIGNER
Book designed by Kate Burgener

EDITOR
Pauli Loeffler

PROOFREADER
Chanel Lyon

AUTHOR
Written by Ronald Huereca

DISCLAIMER
This book contains mature content and is not suitable for all audiences.

CONTENTS

1:	JOAQUIN	1
2:	THE PACKAGE	9
3:	JULIE BRIGGS	16
4:	STELLA	24
5:	EMILY	30
6:	STUART	37
7:	THE PRE-SCREENERS	43
8:	THE CEO	49
9:	THE LEGALITY	55
10:	THE BARISTA	64
11:	REPUTATION DESTRUCTION	71
12:	RENEE	78
13:	MARC	86
14:	THE FALLOUT	95
15:	GOING VIRAL	103
16:	SAMANTHA	109
17:	VERONICA	116
18:	THE COPYCAT	123
19:	REVENGE	132
20:	INFAMY	140
21:	THE INDICTMENTS	153
	EPILOGUE	170
	ACKNOWLEDGEMENTS	173

Chapter 1

JOAQUIN

Joaquin is a prick. His earliest memory was staring at a girl's panties as she climbed up a slide during kindergarten. I guess that made him a fucking sicko pervert-in-training. Start 'em young.

He is the consummate creep. If he even walks in a lady's direction, his eyes glued to the tits and ass of any passerby who is a 2 or above. He doesn't even have to try; he is just naturally a letch. Throw in the fact that he's a tad bit mentally unbalanced... well, you have an all-around fucked up individual.

He's the classic serial killer type. Someone in the neighborhood could be horrifically murdered. Perhaps a night robbery. Joaquin sneaks into the house. The lady reaches for the taser. It misfires. Joaquin grabs the crowbar he used to pry the door open and caves her head in with it.

Hypothetically speaking it could happen. And if it did, let's just say the neighbors would immediately assume it was him.

He's not the sort who'd make the perp walk with some innocent southern-sounding neighbor exclaiming, "Holy hell! No way in tarnation could Joaquin have done this. He's always been so sweet to me and my grandbaby, Irene. Would you like to see a picture?"

Instead, this dude would get the hardcore, all-knowing, wise man, "Hell yeah, that fucker did it! You didn't see it coming? That freak had Dahmer written all over his crazy ass."

And now here is Joaquin, sitting at his computer screen, going over the carnage that is attempting to escape his brain.

He stumbled upon Mindefusement on the darknet. It seemed too good to be true. Just dream of a fantasy. Hire somebody to bring it to life almost Total Recall style. Well, not precisely Total Recall.

Mindefusement works by making customized films. The client, in this case, the prick Joaquin, comes up with the story. In Movieland, I suppose that is the screenplay. Then the story is broken down into more bite-sized pieces that can be choreographed, staged, and acted. So yeah, pretty much like making a short movie.

The way it works is you go to an obscure website, submit an obscene amount of money as a deposit to prove you're not fucking around, and after a thorough background screening to make sure you aren't with law enforcement and can pay up, you're connected to the snooty sales dude.

The sales people, while obviously scum of the earth, are highly trained in the dark arts. How do you sell a fucked up fantasy? You have to take your game to a much higher level.

Let's talk about Jake. He's the sleazy scumbag, money-grubbing, ass-kissing pre-screener AKA sales guy. Imagine a used car salesman combined with a semi-competent insurance agent with the personality of a door-to-door Jehovah's Witness riding on the handlebars of a Mormon's bicycle.

You'd think there would be a special Hell for sales people... and there is. But Jake is not that despicable, right? Well, aside from being in a profession that's too grubby for even a Nicholas Cage character to take on. However, the Jakester was an excellent pre-screener. He can convince the clients to part with their money.

Joaquin was connected with Jake via a Google Hangout after he paid his deposit.

"Hi, Joaquin. I'm Jake. I'm going to explain the process to you. Please consider this a pre-screening, and if this doesn't work out, we'll refund your deposit."

Joaquin was irritated at the prospect of talking to a sales guy. And he didn't understand why he had to be pre-screened.

"What the fuck is this, Jake? You expect me to talk to a sales guy? I already dropped ten fucking grand, and I'm talking to an asshole over a goddamn Google Hangout?"

You see? An obvious prick. And a creeper. Let's not forget that part.

"Joaquin... my man," Jake said as he foolishly tried to

relate to the psychopath.

"I want to talk to someone else," Joaquin interrupted. "Someone who doesn't depend on a commission."

"We don't work on commissions, Joaquin." Jake lied.

Joaquin, growing frustrated, said, "Just give me someone else. Fuck you. I already hate you."

"Like who do you want? My manager?" the Jake laughed. He continued, "What you don't realize is this is a pre-screening. We have to determine if you'll make a good client."

Joaquin's temper was slowly making him into the ideal candidate. He had just dropped a relatively enormous amount of money, and now he was being told he is the one who needs to prove his worthiness. Not exactly Joaquin's cup of tea.

"Okay, sales guy named... Jake," He spat out the name. "You want to know what I think of you?"

Jake remained silent.

"I've already captured your face. It's not hard to do a Google reverse image search. I'll find your profile. Then I'll find your friends. Then I'll find your address. And then I'll find you. And I am itching to use my frequent flier miles. So please let me talk to someone else."

Jake played dumb. He may have met his match and would very likely have had to go back to corporate with a recommendation on how to improve the pre-screening process... if it weren't for the fact this threat had occurred before. Pre-Jake, there was some poor schmuck of a salesman named Lenny. Lenny got fresh with a client, then he foolishly refused to give the client back the $10,000 deposit. The client conveniently tracked poor Lenny down just outside of his apartment and ironically put Mindefusement on the hook for way more than the $10,000 in hospital bills. Something about almost being beaten to death tends to be costly. Now Mindefusement had on-site pre-screeners. As in, a creepy, white panel van stood parked right across the street from the potential client's residence. Inside the van sat the on-site pre-screener and two well-muscled former bouncers ready to take Joaquin for a ride.

Jake didn't want to lose the sale. "Look, Joaquin, we got off on the wrong foot. You are turning out to be a really great candidate, and I think you are the type of client we're looking for." The threat of bodily harm made Joaquin an ideal candidate.

"Great," Joaquin said. "But that doesn't negate the fact I hate you, and I want to talk to someone else."

"There's nobody else to talk to. Let's change topics," Jake said. "You're obviously a good candidate. So we need to talk a torture template."

"Torture template?" Joaquin asked.

"Sorry." Jake chuckled. "It's our internal lingo. Most of the time our clients want some form of torture. So we call what our client comes up with a torture template."

"So you'll take my twisted fantasy without judging me on it like I'm some freak and make it happen in real life?"

"Hold up there Joaquin." Jake held his hand up like a school crossing guard. "We don't do this for real. You do realize that?"

"You think I'm a fucking idiot, Jake?" Joaquin said

starting to get irritated again.

"Of course not!" Jake said, trying to brush it off. "Some clients actually believe we're a hit squad, but you're obviously of superior intelligence," he remarked, thinking just the opposite.

"Cut out the bull shit!" Joaquin retorted heatedly.

"Okay, all I really need to know is what you want us to do for you."

Joaquin thought for a moment. "Okay, there's this girl…" he paused to collect his thoughts as his emotions started to surface. "She won't give me the time of day. I see her nearly every day in the building where I work. I say hello to her and smile at her every time I walk past her. But she never makes eye contact. She just stares at the floor or her phone and won't even look up. It's like I'm not even there."

"I hate that! Happens to me all the time!" Jake lied.

"I want a video of her walking through a crowd of people throwing random shit on her kind of like on Game of Thrones."

"Naked?"

"Yes, but fairly beaten up first."

"So you want her humiliated?" Jake asked.

"Exactly!" Joaquin stated. "This lady needs to pay for every lost smile I attempted to throw at her."

Jake paused. "So let me get this straight. A lady who doesn't give…"

"Who won't even acknowledge my existence," Joaquin interrupted.

"… does a public walk of shame," Jake concluded.

"Yes!" Joaquin exclaimed with excitement.

"Well, it sounds like we have a very do-able torture template, my friend."

"I don't like that phrase: torture template," Joaquin whined.

"We'll call it whatever you want, Joaquin," Jake said.

"Let's just call it 'RBF payback,'" Joaquin suggested.

"RBF? Ha. Resting Bitch Face. I love it!" Jake chuckled. "Well, Joaquin, I'm happy to tell you, you've passed pre-screening, but this is just the start."

"Of what?"

Jake explained: "The process. We'll write a script, hire an actor to play the girl, and come up with a budget for filming."

"And how are you going to find an actor that looks just like this girl?" Joaquin asked.

"Wigs and make-up man," Jake stated matter-of-factly.

"Okay, I see where this is going... And how much do these productions usually cost?"

"These types of movies can start off at about $10,000 a minute, and go up from there for any CGI," Jake replied

Joaquin gasped. For the first time in his life, he realized his psychosis was incredibly expensive and had a sudden realization that perhaps being involuntarily committed was preferable, but he was fixated on making this film: "Well fuck, I guess my trip to the moon can wait."

"So are you in, Joaquin?" Jake asked

Joaquin sighed. He had succumbed to his own sickness aided a bit by Jake's salesmanship, and replied, "Fucking yes, I'm in."

Jake breathed a sigh of relief. Another commission. "Great," Jake said. "You'll receive a welcome package shortly from one of our on-site pre-screeners."

"What!?!" Joaquin exclaimed.

"We cover all our bases, Joaquin. Your package will be delivered shortly. We'll be talking again soon."

Joaquin's doorbell rang just as Jake hung up. Joaquin felt a wave of panic sweep over him as the doorbell rang again: Mindefusement was already at his door. Joaquin realized Mindefusement wasn't a company to fuck with.

Chapter 2
THE PACKAGE

Amanda smiled to herself as she monitored the Google Hangout meeting between Joaquin and Jake. She sat in the passenger seat of the white panel van parked across the street from Joaquin's townhouse. After Lenny's unfortunate incident which cost Mindefusment a small fortune, the company started sending pre-screeners to the client's location to safeguard against any attacks on the salespeople. Frankly, Amanda quite enjoyed dealing with the occasional disgruntled client. She loved to regale the others at Mindefusement with the stories of her personal contacts with the endless variety of people she met as an on-site pre-screener.

Amanda was a Latina version of Lucy Liu. Amanda's long lashes, lovely smile, shiny dark hair, and stunning figure combined with her lilting southern drawl generally mollified the vast majority of irritated or irate clients, particularly male clients. Amanda was always very direct with the client. She wasn't going to take any nonsense or tolerate a runaround. However, dealing with clients in person required a certain look of intimidation and the ability to back it up. Amanda's dark brown eyes had a fire in them that quelled most arguments, and Amanda was trained in a variety of martial arts and was capable of taking care of herself. In addition to Amanda, there were two well-muscled ex-bouncers that remained in the van watching her in case she needed back-up. So far, Amanda had never needed them, but they'd hop out of the van at the first hint of violence, and their mere appearance would be enough to cowl the client should the worst happen.

She exited the white van and strode confidently towards Joaquin's townhouse in Waco. Her trip hadn't brought her that far from Mindefusement's unobtrusive headquarters in Frisco, Texas, so it was a day trip for her. She was in constant contact with her two bodyguards through an earpiece. Just in case a client had weapons or backup, she had the human resources to take over if necessary. And Amanda was kind of hoping for that moment. She wanted that "Instant Karma" she had witnessed on YouTube videos.

Amanda made her way to his door, carefully stepping around the bowls of kibble and water on the porch. Joaquin was socially inept, and the first thing most people felt was instant discomfort caused by an indefinable creepiness in his manner. But Joaquin loved cats and cared for the neighborhood strays. She rang the doorbell once and waited. Silence. She rang the doorbell several times in rapid succession. Joaquin opened the door with a confused and upset look.

"Who the fuck are you?" Joaquin demanded.

Amanda, instead of taking a step backward, she moved towards Joaquin and replied, "I'm from Mindefusement. I have your package here. You are to take it now and follow the instructions when you open the Mindefusement app using the PIN in this envelope. Enter the PIN, and it will prompt for you to register a fingerprint. Just follow the instructions, and you are good to go, sir."

Joaquin stood dumbfounded, not to mention more than a little freaked out by Amanda's appearance on his doorstep in less than a minute after his call with Jake had ended. "I'm not taking your package! I don't want your fucking package! Take your creepy package and get the fuck out! I'm not doing this anymore!"

Amanda, taken aback by the sudden change of heart said in her best sexy, southern drawl, "Oh, well, it's too late to pull out now, honey."

"I'll call the F.B.I." Joaquin threatened.

"Why? We're not doing anything illegal." Amanda stated, not having it. She didn't like the lip from Joaquin. She began to think extortion or blackmail was the way to go with Joaquin's personality.

"Then I'll just call the cops and say you're harassing me!" Joaquin yelled.

"How's that?" Amanda asked, peeved. "Giving you our welcome package? Do you remember the call you were just on? You verbally accepted the terms and conditions of Mindefusement. I heard every word." Amanda continued, "Or how about the recording we now have? The girl you mentioned that we could warn? We already have her name and address."

"Fuck you..." Joaquin breathed unsteadily.

"Look hon'," Amanda said in a serious tone, "Take the package or you can go fuck yourself with your fantasy hard-on. Do you want a refund or the package?"

Joaquin's spirit sank. He took a deep breath and said: "I want the package."

"Then take it!" Amanda said in a frustrated tone.

Joaquin grabbed the package from her outstretched hand, hustled inside, slamming the door behind him.

"Have a nice day!" Amanda yelled sweetly through the closed door. "Asshole," she muttered under her breath.

Inside, Joaquin stared at the package. Was this some Pulp Fiction type briefcase where nobody in their molested mind can ever figure out the contents? Fuck you, Tarantino.

After several hours, Joaquin finally opened the package. Inside was a heavily modified Android touch-screen tablet, an RSA key, and an envelope with the PIN and a letter with additional instructions.

For those not familiar with an RSA key, think of a device you wear on yourself at all times where the code is regenerated periodically. Mindefusement uses a combination of RSA and two-factor security to chat with their clients securely.

The letter read: "After you open the app with the PIN, this tablet will require that you register a fingerprint and a phone number which will serve as two-factor authentication. The tablet will only work with your registered fingerprint and the special RSA key (included in the package). The RSA key shall be kept in a secure location. When both the RSA key and fingerprint are validated, you will receive a text message with a 6 digit code. Once you enter the code, you will be connected immediately to the home screen where you will find the Mindefusement app. Once the app is open, you can connect with a Mindefusement representative, assuming one is available."

Joaquin followed the instructions. He pressed the home button on the tablet, which prompted him for his fingerprint. He scanned his right thumbprint ten times to register it. The tablet then asked for his phone number, which was sent a six digit code to verify the number. The app then asked for his RSA key, which he entered. Within seconds, his phone buzzed signaling the arrival of another 6 digit code. Joaquin entered this code, and the Mindefusement app appeared on his tablet. He opened it.

"Wow, these guys have their shit together." Joaquin thought.

The loading screen immediately popped up with the Mindefusement logo. After several seconds, he saw three choices: Chat, Schedule, and Videos. The Videos button was grayed out as he had none. He was curious, so he clicked on Chat. The app now displayed: "Please wait to be connected to a Mindefusement representative. Your hold time is less than 30 seconds."

Conveniently, Cassandra, a Mindefusement rep, was available for chat. She worked as a form of support technician for the company.

Cassandra was the chipper sort. She's the type of person non-morning people hate because she is running at full steam at the start of the day, while everyone else needs ten cups of coffee to catch up.

Cassandra's smiling face popped up. Joaquin was immediately pleased. Her long Gwyneth Paltrow like hair quickly mesmerized Joaquin.

"Hi, Joaquin," Cassandra said politely. "I'm here to answer any questions you might have."

Joaquin stared at the screen. Cassandra's teeth sparkled brightly like white Greek marble. However, Joaquin wasn't thinking of the Bust of Diana as he quietly bemoaned the fact that he could only see about an inch of Cassandra's cleavage.

Cassandra spoke matter-of-factly, "I'm here to help. Is this your first time?"

Joaquin finally broke his silence, "Yes, I'm not sure what to do."

"Oh, we just talk. I'm here to walk you through your torture template if you have that available."

"I do," Joaquin said, "But I'm still really hazy on what your company does."

"Well," Cassandra replied, "We take that fantasy in your head and turn it into a film you can download and screen for yourself."

"How long does it take for me to get the video?"

"Do you mind sharing your torture template with me? It's been too soon for Jake to have put it into your file."

"Sure. Game of Thrones-style walk of shame for a girl I despise."

"Oh great!" Cassandra said enthusiastically. "I adore that series, and that's one of my favorite scenes!"

Joaquin, thoroughly enjoying contact with this beauty responded: "Yeah, I love Game of Thrones. I'm a bit obsessed with it."

"Me, too. Well, Joaquin, we'll use your deposit to hire a director and actor. More than likely there will be extras and wardrobe, so we try to budget high on things like this so that you aren't surprised with an extra $40,000 or something like that. We also try to prepare you for the higher end of the price range so you don't have sticker shock when we give you the bill."

"Sounds good. When should I log in again?"

"Oh, the app has push notifications, so if you turn those on, we'll update you on progress via that and also via SMS."

"So... how often should I use the package?"

"Anytime you want to talk like we're talking now, or if you want to set a meeting with Jake, we can certainly schedule an appointment."

"Sounds great, Cassandra. I hope to see more of you."

Cassandra smiled and closed the connection. The Mindefusement logo immediately replaced Cassandra on the tablet and he was back to the main screen.

Joaquin had had enough excitement for the day. He closed the app and set the tablet on his computer desk.

Joaquin realized this company was for real and thought of other fantasies he could turn into movies. If only he were rich. Thankfully for the world, Joaquin is just a light-weight with a sick mind. And a cat lover.

Chapter 3
JULIE BRIGGS

Julie grew up in the Dallas area and had a rather prestigious family. Her father was a thoracic surgeon and her mother was a successful lawyer who specialized in corporate mergers. Julie and her younger brother Stuart went to elite private schools where they both excelled academically.

Julie decided to follow in her mother's footsteps after graduating Summa Cum Laude from Southern Methodist University and entered its law school. She did well there and made the Law Review.

She had her pick of job offers from top law firms. Not only was she smart, but she also satisfied a diversity need for the predominantly male law firm that hired her: she was female. Another thing about Julie was that she was easy on the eyes, which did increase her value in dealing with its corporate clients, the vast majority of whom were male.

Stuart, however, did not fare so well. He had some "run-ins" with classmates during high school that were somewhat violent but managed to avoid suspension or expulsion by getting decent grades and his parents' reputational and financial stature. However, shortly before graduation, he was diagnosed as bipolar at the early age of eighteen. His father's connections allowed Stuart to be seen by a top professional well before the average Joe made it to the top of the waiting list for an appointment.

He was kept well under control through medication and therapy. Stuart decided to use his creativity and drive and pursue an art degree at the Rhode Island School of Design. However, with hormones raging and feeling invincible, he went off his medication. He dropped out midway through his sophomore year and moved back to Dallas to live with his sister Julie. At Julie's insistence, he was put back on medication and things evened out.

Then, tragedy struck. Julie and Stuart's world crashed literally when their parents were involved in a head-on car collision that wiped out everyone involved with the exception of a thirteen-year-old. The minor's guardian, as well as the estate and other children killed in the collision, sued Julie and Stuart's parents' estates, and all of the assets of Julie and Stuart's parents were awarded to the surviving child of the accident.

Stuart went off the deep-end so-to-speak and went manic. After an alleged stalking and assault incident, he was placed in the Oxford Behavioral Health Center in the

Dallas area. Lacking funds, Julie did her best to pay for Stuart's treatment and visited him regularly. Her relationship with Stuart and the time needed to maintain it was now becoming a "problem" with Julie's employer.

Late one Friday afternoon, Julie was summoned to the executive senior partner's office. She left her tiny windowless office on one of the lower floors and took the elevator up to the imposing corner office of the partner.

She walked down the long and plush carpet leading to Mr. Hinkley's office which had an expansive view of the city of Dallas. Julie felt a wave of nausea pass over her as her hands became cold and clammy with dread of the conversation to follow.

"You wanted to see me, sir?" Julie asked her boss as she knocked politely and entered his office.

Julie knew why she'd been summoned. It was about her brother Stuart. Stuart's behavior was like an F-5 tornado plowing down the Interstate, not giving a good goddamn who he sucked into oblivion. Because of his mental illness, Stuart, like a tornado had no control or predictability. It wasn't his fault that people got in his way.

"It's either inpatient psych, or you go to jail. You pick." the District Attorney prosecuting the case told Stuart and Julie. Julie did everything she could to fight the court order placing her brother behind locked doors with bored psychiatrists. She felt obligated to use her legal expertise and what funds she had to save his life.

Stuart as a court-ordered "guest" of the psychiatric facility shared bunks with junkies, psychotic people, and those who were suicidal. His college-educated ass and affluent upbringing just didn't mix well with other patients.

"Close the door." Mr. Hinkley ordered.

Julie turned and pushed the door shut by its polished brass handle. It didn't creak, but instead, the click of the lock echoed loudly in Julie's head, reminding her of the mental and physical prison her brother lived in. She instantly felt like that all her co-workers were watching her through the glass walls of the plush corner office, although she couldn't see them. Julie took a deep breath to try to alleviate the knots in her stomach.

"Sit down, please," he requested.

Julie sat down in the overstuffed expensive leather chair and crossed her long legs.

"How are you?" Julie asked a bit too brightly, trying to break the tension in the room.

"I'm afraid we have some bad news."

"We. It's always we. Never someone wanting to take the blame." Julie thought.

"We've been monitoring your performance over the past 90 days, and we think it's time we let you go."

"What?" Julie demanded testily, her worst fear having been realized. She had nothing to lose challenging Mr. Hinkley.

"Your priority has to be our law firm, and you've been distracted and your head isn't in the game. You've missed meetings. You've missed deadlines. Your affection and care for your brother is admirable, but is a real liability for the firm."

"He's ill. You can't fire me because my brother is sick," Julie shouted as dread turned to rage, and breaking her composure. Hot tears of anger streamed down her face.

"We're an at-will employer. And you're being at-willed." her boss stated dryly.

At that point, Julie's anger was typically reserved for the idiots that cat-call her on the way to work, and she reached her breaking point. She, too, became an F-5 tornado as her adrenaline rose.

As eloquent as Julie was, there were no words for this heartless buffoon.

In anger and adrenaline pumping, she took on the strength of a superhero and hoisted the heavy chair and hurled it at her boss. With satisfaction, Julie saw she had lacerated his forehead causing blood to flow and a rapidly growing bump.

Mr. Hinkley stumbled from the impact, blood streaming through his fingers as he searched for his handkerchief before hitting the emergency button located under his desk. Security guards quickly appeared and roughly escorted Julie out of the building.

Although Mr. Hinkley and the firm chose not to press charges for the assault, the incident was talked about in legal circles and her reputation was shot. She had burned her bridges and people viewed her as the same nut case as her brother.

When Julie got passed her abrupt termination from her law firm, she turned her attention to finding other employment to support herself and to take care of Stuart. She checked employment listings, signed up with recruiters, but her reputation preceded her. She was getting nowhere.

Enter Mindefusement. The incident and details of how and why the staid and rational Julie viciously attacked a senior partner made Julie a great prospect for legal counsel for the company.

"Thanks for meeting with us, Julie," the interviewer from Mindefusement said. "So why do you want to work for Mindefusement?"

"Well, to be honest, I couldn't find anything on Google or even on your website about what you all actually do. I really need a good job, and all my training is in the legal field."

"We're into therapeutic remedies. We let people experience their fantasies."

Julie smiled as if she knew exactly what the interviewer was talking about.

"So can we address the elephant in the room?" the interviewer wondered aloud.

Julie looked around and asked innocently, "What elephant?"

After an extended silence, Julie knew the topic was now her brother and the assault on her stupid ex-boss.

"Look, that is behind me. I was in a bad spot." Julie said, confessing.

"And it's also the reason we're sitting on two cozy loveseats too heavy for you to lift, even in anger." the interviewer laughed.

This observation made Julie chuckle out loud.

"Julie, we're a unique company. We focus on those who have fantasies which are better enacted in a movie format."

"And what's your interest in me?" Julie urged.

"We're looking for a lawyer like yourself. We need you to be at the forefront of our business."

"That sounds like long hours and weekends."

"At a minimum." the interviewer stated.

"But..." Julie interrupted.

"Your brother." the interviewer was up-front.

"We need a talented lawyer like yourself, Julie. You're unemployable by a reputable law firm, and don't have the financial wherewithal to open your own firm. So working with us might be your best bet here. But know this, we want to take care of your brother."

"You can't though," Julie said.

"We know of better facilities. Facilities where counseling happens every day, and they're not locked into a room almost 24/7."

The interviewer continued, "We're Mindefusement. We're a barely legal company if we're legal at all. We need a talented lawyer like you to make sure we're still in the barely legal category should we ever be exposed to the public."

"I'm told my brother is a liability."

"Absolutely! But instead of wanting to fire you, we want to hire you. We'll pay you a more than decent salary, and provide you with the additional perk of transferring your brother to a nicer facility."

Julie scoffed, "A nicer facility would be one that has a washing machine, and that's no joke."

"You get to pick where his care will be. How about that?" the interviewer retorted.

Julie thought the offer was too good to be true. It

probably was.

"I need time to process all this," Julie replied.

"Can you process this in 24 hours?" the interviewer said impatiently.

"No way! Are you fucking kidding me?" Julie spat. "I'm desperate for a job, but not that desperate. I want to know more about your company. Right now you're a mystery."

"I thought we already covered that. But we'll let you shadow a client call. How about that?"

Julie thought about it and concluded a shadow never hurt anybody.

"That doesn't sound too bad, actually."

The interviewer said, "You'll find Mindefusement to be a pretty benign company."

"Isn't that for me to decide?"

The interviewer chuckled. "Absolutely."

Chapter 4
STELLA

Julie was seated in the small conference room in front of the laptop screen for her "ride-along" as a shadow. The Mindefusement client in the Google Hangout was Stella.

Stella Davies was a grumpy Brit who immigrated to America about fifteen years ago to practice medicine, specifically, obstetrics and gynecology for which she was board certified. She was an attractive woman in her late-forties with her ice-blonde hair held in a ponytail revealing her high cheekbones and forehead. Stella was unable to have children and had lost two husbands over this. The bitterness of her fate reflected in her eyes. Stella found her "specialty" after her second divorce. She became an abortion doctor. AKA, a baby murderer, depending on your political and religious views. It was her way of getting back at her barren situation. Her internal rage was secretly satisfied by every terminated pregnancy. This had appeased Stella's wrath for a bit, but, over the last few years, it had grown to the point where providing abortions wasn't enough to satiate her anger. Since she couldn't conceive a child, she felt no pregnant woman should be able to give birth, and her obsession with the iniquity of the situation had become her sole focus.

When she heard of Mindefusement, she made a deposit at once. Stella was a repeat customer and had previously commissioned a number of videos. Now she was ready to turn her sickest fantasy into pseudo-reality. As she opened her Mindefusement tablet and entered the Google Hangout, she saw an array of faces ready to grant her wishes.

In the Google hangout, Stella could see familiar faces: Jake and Phil Roth, the director (Phil went by Roth). There was also a third person present, a very pretty unknown female. Each had their own laptop and earbuds.

Jake, who was very familiar with Stella, greeted her enthusiastically: "Stella, it is wonderful to see you again! We are looking forward to..."

Stella interrupted Jake: "Yes, nice to see you and Roth again, but who is the woman?" having had enough of introductory pleasantries and wanting to get right to her new torture template.

"Hello, Dr. Davies, I'm Julie Biggs," Julie said into her mic taken by surprise by Stella's abruptness. Julie thought she was just supposed to be a fly on the wall.

"And what is your purpose here?" Stella inquired.

Julie hesitated momentarily in responding, and Jake jumped in with: "She's my shadow today. She's going to learn the ropes if that's okay with you."

Stella nodded, "Nice to meet you, Ms. Biggs. I'm assuming you are not married?"

Julie spoke up, "No, I'm not married and never have been." Julie paused for a brief second and added: "I have no children and have no plans to have any."

"Indeed," Stella said matter-of-factly.

Roth, the director, spoke, "I understand you enjoyed our last little endeavor, and you requested me specifically."

"Yes, and Jake allowed me to see some of your other work, too. You're my favorite director." Stella's earlier torture templates were gruesome, but nowhere near as grotesque as to what she was suggesting now. Stella continued, "I've selected you, Roth my luv, to film this because you seem extraordinarily capable of achieving the product I desire."

Roth, who had filmed many of Mindefusement's goriest movies, read his note cards: "It says you want a baby cut out of a woman's womb and then burned to death?"

Julie tried valiantly not to flinch as she envisioned the torture template in her mind.

"Exactly!" Stella agreed. Julie was shocked but maintained facial control even as her stomach turned over in disgust. What did Roth and Jake just agree to do?

"And you have no particular actor in mind for the pregnant woman?" Roth continued.

"Well," Stella tapped her cheek a couple of times and said, "I have researched several actresses and find Sarah the most agreeable."

"So slap a fat suit on that bitch and rip out her insides, yes?" Roth suggested.

"I just want exclusive close-ups as the woman's womb is being torn open, the baby being pulled from the gaping hole of the woman, its umbilical cord snipped, then dried with a proper towel, and perhaps given a breath of air. Then douse the little baby with some petrol and set it ablaze."

Julie's composure was lost and her jaw dropped letting forth a gasp. Stella enjoyed Julie's reaction to further details.

Stella continued: "And I want a close-up of that woman screaming next to the charred remains of her ripped out child."

"And," Jake added, "You would like a split-screen view on that? Per your usual?"

"No thank you," Stella replied.

"Excellent. This movie should be just a one to two-minute project. One actor. A lot of dolls. Perhaps a real baby if we can find one. And some zombie-like CGI." Roth stated.

"Oh, and one more thing... if you could just throw in an extra minute for the woman bleeding out, I would be thrilled."

"Absolutely," Jake said without missing a beat.

"Will this cost the same as my other movies?"

Jake looked at the director for comment, and Roth said: "There are a lot more detail and CGI needed here, doctor, compared to your previous projects. We may need several takes, which is a lot of baby dolls. And gasoline."

"Not a problem at all," Stella replied. "As you say in

America, 'Just take my money!'"

"As far as the story, since there will be no dialog, I think we can just go ahead without a script and get this done super fast," Roth piped up.

"Splendid," Stella stated. She hung up the call, and the rest hung up as well.

Jake and Roth looked at Julie for comment. "What in the living fuck did you guys just agree to?" Julie demanded. "What kind of business are you running here?"

"Julie," Roth attempted to mansplain, "We just saved three lives: the woman and baby it'll eventually happen to, and our client who will land in prison or worse should she commit the act in real life."

"How many of these videos has Stella commissioned?" Julie asked, aghast. "And you guys are cool being the mindhunters?"

Jake responded, "Stella is special. She does horrific stuff for her day job. Of course, she's going to come up with horrific stuff for her torture templates."

"I still hate that phrase," Julie stated.

"Torture template, torture template..." Jake teased Julie like a child. "Get used to it."

The interviewer entered the room at that point and prompted Jake and Roth to leave. He confronted Julie. "So what do you think, Julie? Think of your brother. It's time for you to decide."

Julie, frustrated, covered her eyes and slowly ran her hands down her cheeks and took a slow, deep breath before answering.

"This one was just gruesome. Can I shadow at least one

more typical client before making my decision?"

The interviewer thought for a moment and said, "We have Emily coming up. I've read her notes. That one should be more suited for you. Do you have anything else to add?"

"Yes, I don't legally agree with showing clients other client videos. Those videos belong to the client or Mindefusement itself and shouldn't be shared for liability purposes."

"It already sounds like you'll fit in here," the interviewer said, "I'll pass that advice along to the CEO."

The room was silent for a moment as Julie gathered her thoughts.

"So the next video call is scheduled for later this afternoon." the Interviewer said, "Has anybody given you a tour of Mindefusement yet?"

"No," Julie replied.

"Let's do a quick tour and I'll take you out for lunch."

"Sounds great. But after that last call, my appetite may need a bit of urging."

The interviewer laughed, "I understand. Stella is special and perhaps a bit psychotic. Let's go shall we?"

"We shall."

Chapter 5
EMILY

The second potential client Jake pre-screened with Julie as his shadow was Emily. Julie asked for the background on Emily and found that she was a lawyer like herself. Julie surmised that they'd have a lot to talk about on the call.

Emily was a big "Final Destination" fan, which is quite a bit of an understatement. She loved every movie in the franchise, even with all the cheesy death scenes and sub-par acting. However, she was never fully satisfied with the death scenes in the movies and wanted to come up with her own.

It wasn't that Emily felt the death scenes were amateurish or lame. In fact, she really loved several death scenes in the movies. Her favorite movie in the franchise was "Final Destination 2" where there was a big car pile-up at the very beginning when a log truck lost its logs and vehicles and their occupants were crushed and dismembered in the aftermath in an assortment of gory and gruesome ways.

Emily's very favorite death scene was the decapitation scene where some poor lady was trying to exit an elevator when a creepy guy carrying artificial arms with hooks decided to sniff her hair. The hooks got stuck in her hair, and she panicked. She partially exited the elevator, but her head was still trapped inside due to the hooks and her entanglement. The elevator doors closed around her neck and the elevator began to go up. Some of the lady's buddies tried to help her by lifting her body up, but this did do no good only delaying the inevitable. With her body danging outside the elevator, she struggled to get the elevator door open with her freed arms, screaming all the way. She screamed frantically until her head was finally separated from her body by the pressure of the elevator when it hit the ceiling outside the elevator doors. The passengers in the elevator were horrified by the decapitated head. Her buddies on the other side of the elevator door hit the floor holding her headless and lifeless torso.

Her second favorite death scene was in "Final Destination 3." She loved the home improvement store scene. She laughed hysterically when the red-headed girl was blown backward against a nail gun, which promptly blasted at least a dozen nails through her skull and hand, causing a painful death.

Running a close third, Emily treasured the infamous pool scene in "The Final Destination" where karma literally bites him in the ass. This douche walks by an obnoxious kid with a water cannon who sprayed him and ruined the guy's phone. The asshole confiscated the water cannon from the kid and threw into a storage area, which accidentally turned the pool's drain on. After an errant golf ball from a nearby golf course hits the douche, he drops his lucky coin. The coin rolls into the pool where it is quickly sucked into the drain. When he dove into the pool to get it, he is sucked ass first onto the drain. He tries to escape and screams for help underwater, but with no success. The suction from the drain rapidly increases and eventually rips his internal organs out and sprays them onto the sidewalk near the drain pressure gauge.

An honorable mention is the crushing glass scene after a poor boy is almost asphyxiated at the dentist. You can see the boy crushed in vivid detail. Emily giggled when this occurred.

With these death scenes in mind, Emily figured that Mindefusement could finally give her the ultimate death fantasy she desired.

She began the pre-screening process with Jake and Julie.

"Hello, Emily," Jake said cheerfully. "I'm Jake, and I'm going to walk you through our pre-screening process. Julie is joining us on this call."

"Hi, Jake and Julie!" Emily said enthusiastically.

"What we're doing today is determining whether you would make a good Mindefusement client," Jake stated matter-of-factly.

"Oh, I will!" Emily smirked. She continued, "So I assume you're a sales guy Jake. What's Julie's role in this process?"

Julie spoke up, "I'm shadowing the call to determine if I want to represent Mindefusement as legal counsel."

"Oh!" Emily exclaimed excitedly, "You're a lawyer like me!"

"Yes," Julie replied, "But non-practicing at the moment. How about you?"

"I have my own firm. I mostly represent people with DUI issues. It's very lucrative because there are always plenty of morons who drink and drive."

"I see," Julie said softly, her mind flashing back to her parents' tragic deaths in that fatal car wreck.

"Ahem." Jake interrupted bringing Julie back to the present. "Shall we get into your notes, Emily? Sorry, I don't want to take you away from your lucrative law practice any longer than I have to."

"Right," Emily said in a more serious tone.

"So," Jake asked, "It says in your notes that you're super into 'Final Destination'?"

"Yes!" Emily eagerly confirmed, "So much so that I have 'Final Destination' tattooed on my upper arm. That way I can hide it from clients. But my boyfriend loves it!"

Jake, surprised, said, "Wow, that's some dedication."

"I love all the films. I don't see them as horror films. I view them as outrageously funny comedies."

She continued, "I had a friend over, and she HATED horror movies. I explained to her to look at the film and death scenes as comedy. It completely changed her perspective on the movies. We binged them all that night."

"So what's your favorite movie?" Jake asked.

Emily thought. "It's definitely Final Destination 2.

Although the first and third ones are close seconds."

"Is that the one where there's a huge pile-up?"

"Yes, that one was the scariest for me. I still can't drive behind a semi-truck filled with logs."

"Wow, you know your 'Final Destination' films," Jake concluded.

"It's kinda like '1000 Ways to Die' for me. The entire series is just one laugh after another for me. It's my 'World's Funniest Videos' but with a lot more blood and guts."

"That's great," Jake said. "So what can we do for you?"

Emily was silent for a moment.

"I want this epic death scene that will outdo all other 'Final Destination' deaths."

Jake, intrigued, asked, "So what's your fantasy?"

"Okay, so I live in Oklahoma where the tornadoes come sweeping down the plains and shit."

"Yeah, we have tornadoes here, too."

"Well anyways, I want some guy pumping gas right in the path of a tornado. At the same time, there is also a liquid nitrogen truck filling up." Emily continued, "So a severe wind gust hits the gas station and topples the liquid nitrogen truck, splitting it in two, spilling its contents on the patrons pumping gas."

"And?" Jake asked, trying to get Emily to elaborate.

"Well, the liquid nitrogen freezes the poor douchebag pumping gas from the waist down. Then the gas station explodes when the tornado hits. The guy dies from being frozen from the waist down and burned to death waist up."

"Holy shit," Jake said, "Yes, that would be a great 'Final Destination' death!"

"Right?!" Emily said smiling confidently.

Jake became serious: "Well, something like this will be pretty pricey."

Emily balked at the mention of funds. "I don't care. I want this death scene so bad. People won't stop drinking and driving. I have lots of clients. I'll camp at DUI checkpoints and hand out cards if I have to. I can't get the scene out of my head."

"Alright, Emily, we'll accept you as a client. A Mindefusement package will be delivered to you shortly."

"Fucking fantastic!" Emily exclaimed. "I can't wait to see what you all come up with."

"Let's keep in touch Emily. I like your style." Jake smiled to himself.

"For sure," Emily said.

Jake and Julie hung up from the call and Emily anxiously awaited her package, which arrived moments later via Amanda. It was another day trip for her.

Jake and Julie sat silently in the small conference room. Jake, breaking the uncomfortable silence, asked, "So how was that one?"

Julie thought out loud, "Compared to the last one? Pretty benign."

"So are you in our out?" Jake asked.

"I think I have made my decision." Julie paused. "It's a yes."

Jake smiled broadly and slapped Julie on the back, "Great, it'll be great to have you on our team and our side. I know the CEO wants to see you on your way out."

"That's fine," Julie stated.

Having come to a decision was a relief, and Julie hurried to the meeting with the CEO to personally accept the job offer. He welcomed her to the company. Her first assignment was a presentation to Mindefusement's Board of Directors on the legality of the company's enterprises. Julie replied, "I'll be happy to do so after I spend some time on research. Also, I want to make a visit to my brother first and give him the news."

"I'm a man of my word, Julie." the CEO stated. "We'll move your brother wherever you want and as soon as possible."

"Great."

"Glad to have you on board."

Chapter 6
STUART

Because Stuart's family was well-to-do, they were able to keep his illness mostly under wraps. Medication helped, and so did therapy — up to a point. But he was a teenager, and like most teenagers with raging hormones, it was difficult, if not impossible, for him to maintain his temper and psychotic breaks with reality.

However, at age 20, tragedy struck when his parents were killed. He had a psychotic break and went back to Dallas to live with his sister Julie.

Stuart, now back on his meds and a recluse at heart, suddenly became highly social. He came out of his shell and became very interested in the opposite sex. In a sense, Stuart became the pubescent teen that he never was; he went manic.

Stuart's trip to the mental facility was precipitated by

his obsession with a married woman named Denise he worked with at his entry-level job with a startup doing graphic design. Denise confided to him that she felt trapped and suicidal in her marriage, and her husband threatened her with violence.

After Denise was absent from work for two days, Stuart's concern turned into an obsession. He texted her over and over with no response. He was very close to calling emergency services to go to her home. Instead, he went over to her husband's work to confront him.

Security refused to admit him into the building, and Stuart turned hostile. The three overweight security guards quickly wrestled him to the ground, handcuffed him, and called the police. At the police station, it was obvious he was psychotic, and he was shipped off to a mental facility for observation for the requisite 72 hours under state law.

Julie was contacted as his next of kin. Stuart was scheduled for a mental health determination in court. Julie conferred with the very junior Assistant District Attorney handling the mental health hearing. He indicated that the examining physician was going to recommend commitment, but he was leaning toward criminal charges. The Assistant District Attorney presented Julie with two choices: jail time for assault and trespassing, or indefinite confinement in a mental health facility assuming Stuart doesn't get better.

Faced with the choices, Julie talked privately with Stuart. Heavily medicated with Zyprexa, Depakote, and Xanax to control his psychosis, Julie did her best to explain the situation to her brother, but Stuart's blank look and inability to communicate did nothing to reassure Julie that he understood the seriousness of the situation he was in. When they appeared before the judge, Julie, as counsel of record, agreed to Stuart's commitment to Oxford Behavior Health Center in Dallas for treatment, and the Assistant District Attorney agreed to drop the criminal charges.

Oxford Behavioral Health Center might as well been named involuntary rehab as it was full of people going through withdrawal symptoms and had a mandatory detox, which was its specialty. The state facility was not designed to treat long-term psychosis and the mentally ill, although the vast majority of those interred there were mentally ill rather than addicts or criminals.

The facility was housed in a dilapidated building, screened by a high hedge in front of an impressively high stone wall. There was nothing to indicate to the people outside that the patients were being held prisoner essentially against their will. Next to the gated entry was a small gatehouse with a security guard. The security guy accepted bribes, and the patients would use him to transport caffeine and nicotine into the facility, which was strictly forbidden.

One night during group therapy, the suicidal residents started sharing their war stories.

"See, I did it the right way, but I'm still here," said a brunette lady, showing off bandages on both of her arms. She had indeed cut her wrists the right way: vertical from wrist to elbow. She did both arms somehow and yet manage to live (she did it in front of her husband during an argument and he called 911 immediately). Just a few days earlier, she freaked out the nurses when she started pulling stitches out with her teeth. She was heavily medicated after that, and this was her first time back in the group in a week.

Another "inmate" said he called 911 before his suicide attempt so that he would be found within a reasonable time frame (e.g., not rotting days later or eaten by insects and rodents). He slit his throat in the bathtub, and a deputy just happened to be close by when the alert came in and saved his life.

A third patient had downed a bottle of bleach. Another one foolishly tried to off herself by taking a month's prescription of Ambien which just caused her to sleep for a few days. One man had decided to hang himself but botched the job when the cord broke. He was found unconscious by his roommate. The blood vessels in his face had burst, and he looked like an alien with a bad case of smallpox.

Another lady spoke of how she wasn't suicidal but threatened to kill someone over the phone. It was either jail or the looney bin for her.

Family day occurred once a week, and Stuart looked forward to it. His sister Julie often brought him clean clothes and entertainment in the form of non-fiction books, which Stuart enjoyed. His favorite book was Flyboys by James Bradley.

When family day was near, the nursing staff all acted as if they suddenly cared. Wounds were treated. Floors were scrubbed. And everybody acted like the Stepford Wives. Then once everyone left, the staff would return to being Mr. Hyde.

Julie and Stu met in the visitor's area. Julie had brought a few books for him to read. Julie hesitated before asking in a baby voice, "I need to ask you, bro... are you happy here?"

Stuart stared at the table as he answered: "No. I hate it here. Most of the time, I'm terrified. I'm harmless compared to the majority of the patients here. I'm just bi-polar. I'm fine when I'm on my meds."

"Is the psychiatrist treating you well?" she asked.

"No," Stuart said candidly, "She thinks I'm just faking it."

"What if I could give you a way out?"

"What do you mean?" Stuart asked.

"I've received an offer from a company based here in the Dallas area. They said they'd help you out as a perk of employment. Get you a better facility. You know, where the psychiatrist cares."

"What, a commune in Colorado where I can stay high 24/7?"

Julie shrugged and grinned. "I doubt that, but I might be able to negotiate it at some point. They seem to really want me, and I've accepted the job."

"Then count me in, sis," Stuart said.

"Okay. Mindefusement is the name of this company, and they had me shadow a few calls, one of which was really gruesome, but I accepted nonetheless."

"What's Mindefusement?" Stuart asked, his curiosity piqued.

Julie responded, "Let's just say, the clients of the company deserve to be in here as much if not more than you do. But if working for them gets you to a better place,

I think it's worth it."

Stuart's eyes welled up with tears, "I love you, sis."

He looked up at Julie with his caring brown eyes. "How long until I get out of this hell hole?"

Julie replied. "Probably within a week, maybe ten days at the most."

He sobbed, "I hate the people here so much. Everyone works against you. The nurses. The doctors. Even the other patients. We don't even get nice beds. How ironic is that?"

"Yeah, they need you to sleep, but give you the flimsiest and cheapest mattresses available."

Stuart got up. They embraced tightly, then Julie walked out of the dingy facility with the knowledge that life was either going to get dark very quickly, or maybe actually work out for both of them.

Julie had the means to help her brother. Stuart was shipped off to a better facility in the Dallas area a few weeks later.

Chapter 7

THE PRE-SCREENERS

To understand what the pre-screeners do, it's useful to consider them in the context of soccer players. The pre-screeners have an impossible task; they're the forwards and goalkeepers for both teams at the same time. These poor dudes are the in the direct line-of-fire of clients, and I'm talking about fuckers worse than the scariest John Malkovich character you've ever seen.

Then there are the on-site pre-screeners. Unfortunately, they've been a necessity since the Incident.

The resulting fallout convinced the Mindefusement leadership to start hiring on-site pre-screeners should the client decide he wants to go all Internet Jay and Silent Bob. The worst happened with Lenny when a client beat him up.

And don't think for a minute that Mindefusement stood still after Lenny's brush with a client. A few hired hands visited the client. The client was given his $10,000 refund and then forced to swallow several Alka-Seltzer downed with hydrogen peroxide with a prompt pounding to the stomach to induce vomiting. I can't imagine it was pleasant.

Now pre-screening is a lot less dramatic, and there's less of a need to intimidate the clients. However Jake had an active threat against him since his last pre-screening, and his co-worker and sometimes lover, Amanda, wanted to gossip.

Amanda, an on-site pre-screener, having just got back from her latest job with Joaquin in Waco, walked into the company break room and immediately stood over Jake. Jake was in the middle of shoveling an atrocious, partially wilted spinach leaf into his mouth. He could stand to lose a bit of weight, and his nagging wife insisted on packing him a salad for lunch.

"Your wife making you eat that shit again?" Amanda chuckled.

"Shut the fuck up Amanda," Jake said in his Dallas-Texas drawl he tries to hide during sales calls.

"Well," Amanda wiggling her hips seductively said, "I have some news about Joaquin."

Jake's interest in the salad, if already pretty nonchalant, moved into the abysmal category reserved for... well, eating rat shit.

Amanda continued, "Hate to tell you this, but, eh, Joaquin had buyer's remorse when I showed up at his door."

"You're kiddin' me, right? What are you talkin' about buyer's remorse?" Jake demanded. "He's the one who told me he was going to Google search me."

"Yeah..."

"Isn't it your job to pre-screen and scare the shit out of our clients?"

Amanda didn't like Jake's tone. He sits behind a computer screen, while Amanda has to carry her anti-rape taser and meet the clients. "You're the pre-screener," Amanda stated. "I showed up. You approved him. And I'm standing there with his welcome package, and he looks at me, and he says 'Oh, no, no, no!'"

Jake, starting to feel sympathetic, said, "Was he as much of an asshole as he was on Hangout?"

Amanda scoffed, "Oh, hell yeah! And..."

Jake interrupted, "Did that guy give you the rape kinda complex?"

"N-n-n-no..." Amanda shook her head while stammering, "It wasn't one of that rape kinda vibes. Although he is very creepy. He looked at me like, 'Oh, no, I changed my mind!'"

Amanda continued, exaggerating a bit, "I looked him dead in the eyes behind my sunglasses. Not sure how good that did. And I said, sorry Joaquin, but, hey, you signed up. Here's your package. You wanna pull out? It's a little bit too late, and you didn't use a condom."

Jake laughed.

Amanda continued reenacting the story, "Here ya go! You take this. And no we're not giving you that money back. It's paid. Now you have a choice..."

Jake interrupted again, "Now I imagine Joaquin put up a little fight at that."

"Well," Amanda explained, "He seemed a bit miffed about it. But as I put it to him, I said, we keep this confidential when you go through with the deal."

Jake asked facetiously "So what was his whole buyer's remorse thing? Let's go back to that. Why did he want to back out all of a sudden? Was it your intimidating 5'3" figure?"

"No." Amanda laughed. "That wasn't it. He just realized..."

"...Or maybe it was the two bouncers sitting in the white van behind you?"

Jake loves to hear himself talk. Like all salesman I suppose.

"No." Amanda continued to laugh. "It wasn't the stupid protein-infused bouncers. He couldn't even see them anyways." She continued, "Truthfully it may have been..."

"Did he see your pistol?"

She ignored the question, "...I looked him in the eye. I said, you know, Joaquin, the thing about it is you spilled your guts, and we've recorded it. We keep this stuff confidential, but there are other ways we can get back at you."

"Oh, you did not!" Jake laughed.

"Oh, hell yeah!" Amanda confidently stated. She continued, "You, Joaquin, gave us your deepest darkest fantasy and..."

"In fairness, he didn't give us any details. We're still developing the storyline." Jake said interrupting yet again like the douchebag he is.

"He gave us what he was looking at as far as that Game of Thrones bitch."

Jake thought for a moment. Amanda was definitely brilliant.

"He did give us enough information, so we have a head's up. We can throw a restrainin' order on his ass, and that'll be easy as pie considerin' we have a few judges in our pockets."

"Yeah, we can probably take him pretty much out of society. Or have him end up on a sex offender registry. But the main thing here was the poor little shrimp Joaquin shivering there..."

"Are you kiddin' me? You made Joaquin squirm?"

Amanda was obviously proud.

"You made the douchebag of all douchebags... squirm?"

Amanda laughed uncontrollably, "Your douche game is strong."

"Yeah, we're not in the gutter. We are the gutter."

After barely recovering, she laughingly said, "Oh, hell! He's nothing! I could squish something like him under my foot in a New York minute. Or a Dallas minute I suppose."

"Even looking at him gives me the Kim Kardashian Paris robbery post-traumatic-stress-disorder syndrome."

"Wow." Amanda paused. "I wouldn't go that far. But close. Yes. But I eat people like that for breakfast."

She continued, "He's trying to tell me to 'Go away. Go away from me. Get away. I'm done with this! No! This is not something I want! I will have the FBI on you!' And I'm looking at him..."

"Let me guess Amanda... You're wantin' a commission out of this dadgum sale, huh?"

"No!" Amanda screamed defensively. "I got a lot of

FUN out of this one. That's worth way more than any kind of money. Dealing with dirtbags and putting them in their place. And then watching how bad they take it when I hand them their package."

She continued, "And you'll receive a bill in the mail. And if you don't pay it, you'll see me again. And I'll have two taller clones with me." She paused and made her best Schwarzenegger impression: "I'll be back."

"Amanda," Jake said laughing, "Even though sometimes I refer to you as that lovable cunt..."

"Fuck you," Amanda said proudly. "And don't use that word. It's rude."

He continued, "I think we need to visit the nap room. Again."

"Are you married today?" Amanda smirked.

"Not today." Jake grinned, showing that his wedding band was missing from his left hand. "I took it off to eat, but I can keep it off if you have something else in mind for me to eat during lunch."

Amanda paused, and then smiled, "You're a fucking pervert, Jake. I definitely expect a commission now."

Chapter 8

THE CEO

The CEO, George Shiner, started Mindefusement roughly two years ago. He did it out of his shame for the odious crime committed by his son, Richard, and the guilt he felt at being unable to prevent it. His second child was a daughter named Renee. She was a model student, and other than disagreeing with Renee's choice to pursue a degree in dramatic arts, they had a good relationship while she was growing up. George agreed to pay Renee's tuition, but she was on her own for room and board.

The CEO and his children weren't exactly new money. The CEO had a rather large inheritance from oil-rich land and land rights originating from his grandfather, Alex Shiner. Alex married Delores, a debutante, the only child of a cattle baron holding several thousand acres in West

Texas where oil was struck. Delores had a head for business, but Delores' father didn't believe that she could hold her own with men in the business world, so he left his vast holdings to his son-in-law, Alex. Delores' job was to entertain Alex's business partners and produce an heir. Unfortunately, Delores only had one child, a daughter, before she drank herself to death from boredom in her early thirties.

The daughter, Alexandra Shiner, became pregnant as a junior in boarding school, and returned home only to die in childbirth producing George Shiner. From an early age, Alex Shiner took George under his wing and included him in his business meetings and negotiations. George was a quick learner. When Alex Shiner passed away at sixty-two from complications of diabetes, his grandson son George was more than ready to take over the family holdings.

Women flocked to George because of his money, but he chose wisely. He and his wife, Amy, raised their children Richard and Renee together for eleven years, but she too passed away at an early age from a heart attack. Even before Amy's death, Richard was a problem. To say that Richard was always a brat would be an understatement akin to saying the destruction of Pompeii was a small barbecue. He committed petty theft, vandalism, experimented with drugs, and killed the family cat. Nothing George had tried seemed to work with Richard. By the time Richard was twenty, he was even more heavily into drugs, and George tried several times to get Richard to stick with rehab and therapy.

Richard had his demons and acted on them. A horrific

crime that rocked the community of Denton, Texas, was perpetrated by "Rick the Blade." Richard, a self-entitled asshole who repeatedly displayed sociopathic behavior throughout his life finally went down for taking it too far.

A coked-up Richard went out of his mind and committed a gruesome crime. He went to the neighbor's house when the husband wasn't home. He dragged Donna, the wife, to the kitchen and tied her up to the butcher block table and gagged her. He used a handy knife to rip open her denim shorts and began raping her. When she continued struggling, he stabbed her in the gut. The couple's three-year-old son, Andrew, was hiding under the dining room table, clutching his favorite stuffed dinosaur during this gruesome act.

Richard finally got bored and sliced her throat and let her choke to death on her own blood. In his drug-induced state, he didn't even try to cover up the crime with his DNA evidence all over the crime scene. Donna's husband returned to find little Andrew squalling at the front door and covered in his mother's blood. The father, Mike, rushed to the child and checked to see what was wrong with him. Then he discovered his wife's raped and mutilated body in a large pool of blood on the butcher block. Mike began screaming, and one of the other neighbors called 911. Mike refused to let go of Andrew as authorities approached.

With public pressure mounting over the grisly crime, authorities were quick to prosecute Richard. Because he was white and affluent, Richard escaped the death penalty. It was determined that Richard would spend the rest of his life behind bars with no chance of parole.

George was devastated. He couldn't believe his nearest and dearest next of kin could commit such a disgusting act. He felt he could've prevented Richard's crime somehow. The only thing he could think of was that if Richard had had an outlet to calm the demons, perhaps the crime would have been averted. Richard's crime was the inspiration for Mindefusement. George was also concerned about Andrew, the traumatized adolescent thirteen-year-old.

This is why George formed Mindefusement. He bought an empty warehouse in Frisco, Texas and moved to the Dallas area. He converted the space in the abandoned warehouse to some movie sets and the rest of the space for offices. He began pursuing filmmakers and actors to allow people to live out their aberrant and dark fantasies through a film, rather than subject real victims to their twisted thoughts.

He envisioned Mindefusement as a secret company but didn't mind if it became mainstream. He wanted to help people. Mindefusement was successful from the start and made enough money so that George could anonymously set up a college fund for Andrew to use when he graduated high school.

George's first hires were the director Roth and a sales guy named Lenny. Lenny conveniently lived in the Dallas area, and Lenny, coming from a marketing agency background, was incredibly talented at getting people to part with their hard-earned cash. Lenny also was familiar with someone who knew the ins and outs of the dark web. Between Lenny and his colleague, Mindefusement drew in clientele.

Mindefusement started advertising for actors and extras in the Dallas area. Mindefusement began to make their first few films with great success. Some actors stayed on as permanent employees, while others were used on a contract basis.

The CEO wanted Mindefusement to be a legitimate and legal company, so he sought out a lawyer he could bring onto the team, which was hard to find given the nature of the business. This lawyer turned out to be the more-than-competent but down on her luck Julie Biggs.

George was a micro-manager and almost always attended the Mindefusement meetings and had the final vote on any new ideas presented. He also had the power to reject clients, which he did occasionally.

After Lenny was assaulted by a prospective client, George made sure Lenny received the best medical care available. However, Lenny refused to return to Mindefusement after the assault. With Lenny gone, the CEO hired Jake as the new sales guy and began doing on-site pre-screening of clients to prevent what happened to Lenny from happening again, even though the extra expense hurt his profit margins.

Regarding movie quality, George strove to be like the late Stanley Kubrick in making sure the quality of the films were suitable for the big screen. As a result, he hired technical staff that specialized in CGI effects, competent directors, and skilled actors.

George knew Mindefusement would grow by word-of-mouth (e.g., underground social media) and had several long-term clients such as Stella. He wanted to prevent another Richard incident and felt giving clients an outlet ultimately saved lives. Mindefusement was initially only found through the darknet, but George wanted to open Mindefusement to more mainstream clients, but worried Mindefusement might outgrow itself. After all, he knew that everyone has a breaking point.

With Mindefusement, George felt he could provide relief to clients wanting to live out their fantasies without real-life criminal action. He was delighted with the current success rate and cherished the management of the company and felt it was in good hands with his current staff.

Chapter 9

THE LEGALITY

The Board of Directors of Mindefusement met in the main conference room. It was a windowless room with a V-shaped, glossy mahogany conference table surrounded by comfortable, cushy executive-level chairs. The dove grey walls were decorated with colorful abstract art to alleviate the feeling that the Board of Directors was meeting in a bunker. At the tip of the V, stood a podium. To the left and right of the podium were matching HD screens in case someone needed to present videos or PowerPoints.

Julie Biggs, General Counsel for Mindfusement, was asked to provide a presentation on the legality of the company. As her first meeting with the Board, she was enthusiastic to present and prove her worth to the company. She stood behind the podium, smiling brightly trying to still her nervous energy. The members of the Board sat quietly and waited for her to speak.

"As most of you know, I am the newly hired General Counsel for your company. It's a pleasure to meet you. I'm here today to talk about the legality of the company..." Julie took a deep breath to start her prepared speech with a winning smile.

Julie continued, "Mindefusement as far as my review of the company's records has gone, hasn't committed any crimes. That being said, the issues we are concerned with are in the areas of contract and tort law. I know contract law is a real snooze, but I'll cover that first because what is in the contract bears directly on the company's possibly tort liability."

"Mindefusement needs an iron-clad contract with indemnity and hold harmless provisions with regard to client's use of the video other than for his or her own personal enjoyment. No sharing with others without specific written permission from our company. The videos will be copyrighted and will display the FBI warning regarding criminal and civil liability statements we all fast forward through when we rent or buy a movie," Julie paused as those present looked at each other in surprise.

Jake piped up: "We have always allowed the clients to do whatever they want with the movies we create for them. After all, they are paying a minimum of ten grand for us to film their torture templates."

Julie responded sharply, "That practice is going to end immediately if the company wants to avoid tort liability. In reviewing the contract, there is a provision that

Mindefusement retains all rights to the use and the distribution of the product. This easily permits the company to add the FBI warning and gives the company the power to amend the terms of use under the contract. Adding the indemnity and hold harmless clauses, however, are meaningless if the client does not have the ability to pay costs and attorney fees in defending Mindefusement in any action against caused by the video produced for the client."

The CEO and Chairman of the Board jumped in: "We already do extensive background reports on potential clients including pulling credit reports during the pre-screening process."

Julie sighed silently, "That is great except pulling a consumer credit report without the consumer's explicit consent violates the Fair Credit Reporting Act in most situations."

The CEO replied, "When the user requests more information about Mindefusement through the website, he or she must supply several pieces of information: name, home and employment, addresses, annual income, citizenship, age, and social security or citizen ID number. There is a checkbox with terms-of-service that the user must agree to that discloses all of this information including consent to pull a credit report."

Julie replied, "Good to know. That being said, pre-screening needs this information up front and Mindefusement's accounting department will have to evaluate the potential customer's financial wherewithal before any pre-screening takes place. If the customer does not meet the requirements for whatever reason,

Mindefusement must advise the customer of the reason for denial, and if the denial is based on information in the credit report, it must advise of the reason for denial and supply the name and address of the credit reporting agency to allow the consumer to dispute the information."

"I'm sorry, but basically I am a salesman, and all this talk of indemnity clauses and credit reports just went way over my head," Jake whined.

Julie, provided Jake and the other non-lawyers with an example, "Say we're in the skydiving business. Before someone jumps out of a perfectly good airplane, we would have them sign a contract with hold harmless and indemnity clauses that they understand the risks involved during the skydive. This protects the skydiving company should injury or death occur that is not due to negligence of the company."

"So an indemnity clause protects us from what our clients might do with the video?" Jake asked.

"Exactly!" Julie exclaimed.

Jason, in charge of the Mindefusement website, its app, and security, was a new-hire like Julie. He interrupted, "We already have clients digitally sign a contract before production starts. The Mindefusement app allows clients to export their videos to Dropbox, Amazon AWS, and other services so they can view them on their hardware of choice rather than solely available on the package. What happens when someone inevitably posts their video to YouTube for public consumption or their storage account gets hacked and the video is leaked?"

"Going forward, the client will be restricted to viewing

the video solely on the package. The package has strong two-factor authentication and will be the only means for the customer to access his or her video. It even has an HDMI port, correct, so the client can view it on any screen? Granted, we can't prevent the customer from playing the video on the package for others or using a camera to record it on another device, but pirating is a problem across the entertainment industries."

Julie paused and then asked, "How many current clients do we have that may have downloaded the videos to other services? And, do we have any way to know if a client has done that?"

Jake replied, "We have about fifty clients. I'm not IT, so I can't answer your second question. Maybe Jason can."

Jason responded, "We track exports in the app, and so far ten or so have done an export to a third-party service through our tracking software. However, we don't have any records if a client has shared a video publicly. To adhere to your request, I'll have to update the app to prevent any further exports."

"So, basically the company is hanging out there with possible liability due to twenty percent of our clients who may have copies of their torture templates stored on off-site services?" Julie said. After a pregnant pause and seeing the looks of horror on the faces of the directors, she continued, "There is very little we can do about these at this point other than personally visit each of the clients, explain a change in policy, offer them an additional torture template either free or at a reduced price in consideration of signing a new contract which will indemnify and hold the company harmless from liability for prior videos. Now whether the customers actually will sign or not is their choice and out of our control."

The CEO said, "Get the exports off the app immediately, Jason. And Jake, you're in charge of getting the clients to sign the new contract."

"That's a lot of work," Jake said sighing. "So we need to inform the clients that spent hard money that the video isn't really theirs and they share at their own risk?"

Jason added, "I can do some damage control and 'encourage' the clients to sign the revised contract if I yank the videos from the app until they agree to sign."

"That'll work better than contacting each client individually," Jake said with relief.

The CEO ranted: "We don't want to piss off those clients! Disabling viewing if the client has already uploaded the video to YouTube but kept it private may just be the trigger for them to make it public. This situation needs to be taken care of as discreetly as possible treating the client with kid gloves."

"Fine, it's going to be legwork for me then," Jake concluded. "I'll revisit each client that has shared their video with third-party services, have them agree to a new contract, and ask with my sly salesmanship to remove any videos hosted on third-party services."

"That sounds doable," Julie replied.

"So we also need the other eighty percent to sign new contracts as well?" Jake asked.

"Yes, we need them to review the new contract and agree to it This is relatively easy and won't require Jake to move out of his chair. Just like iTunes, the clients will have to review and consent to the revised contract with the hold harmless and indemnity clauses and use restrictions before they can access the video." Julie replied.

Jason replied, "Yeah, I'll just tweak the app to have the new contract pop up prior to watching any more videos. Jake, I'll give you a list of the clients who have shared with third-party services so you can coax them before I make the app changes go live. But I can remove the sharing service right away. I can work on it and release the update after the meeting."

"But if Mindefusement owns the films, won't we be the ones who are sued should something come up?" Jake asked trying to understand.

Julie explained, "I can't prevent Mindefusement from being named in a lawsuit, but we can take steps to protect the company in the event a lawsuit is inevitably brought against us. The contract can shift the financial liability to the client who will be responsible for any financial damages in the event of legal action including an action alleged to be the result if a video is publicly released."

"That sounds rather harsh from the client's end," Jason interjected.

Julie, growing frustrated, replied, "You asked me how to make Mindefusement legal and how to protect Mindefusement. The videos are the inner thoughts of the clients, and there are no legal restrictions on a person's thoughts, opinions, or beliefs as long as they do not result in illegal activity or actions. The point is that the product is the company's, and our goal is to prevent the product from being the cause of illegal activity or actions. We have no choice but to force our clients into a new contract to protect ourselves legally."

The CEO weighed in: "Julie's right. We can be sued to high heaven should a video somehow be leaked, whether it's an internal leak or the client posting the video publicly."

Jake asked, "So hypothetically, what if a client has already published a video publicly?"

Jason thought for a moment, "If we can find it, we can file a DCMA request to have the video removed. But that doesn't stop any re-sharing because after all, the Internet is the Internet, and once it's there, it's out there forever. Are you aware of any public videos?"

"No, but then I haven't been looking for them. And so far, I haven't had a client say, 'My friends loved the video' or brag about the number of hits on YouTube," Jake responded.

Julie asked, "Is there a copyright notice on the videos?"

"No, not currently," Jake replied.

"We need to add one immediately. How quickly can we re-process all the videos to add the notice?"

"We're talking about dozens of videos…" Jason said in a frustrated tone.

The CEO shifted his position in his cushy chair, and made the judgment call, "Let's get it done. Update the app. Add the copyright notice. Have the clients sign new contracts. Remove the videos if we have to get the client's attention. We have to make sure we're protected legally, and I believe Julie has made her points quite clear."

Julie nodded approvingly at the CEO's decision.

"Is there any other business we need to discuss before we conclude this meeting?" the CEO asked.

The room sat silent.

"Alright then. Meeting adjourned. Great job Julie."

Chapter 10

THE BARISTA

Everyone has their pet peeves, right? Well, Antoine has a doozy. He despises it every time someone mispronounces his name.

Antoine, a closet narcissist, had a rather poor upbringing in a Las Vegas suburb. He remembered sleeping on the floor of his mother's apartment on a pallet of blankets because there wasn't a mattress for him. It was just a sacrifice he had to make as a youngster because his mother couldn't afford basic necessities because of her gambling addiction.

According to his mom, Antoine's father was apparently on a remote island somewhere. His father wasn't in the picture of Antoine's upbringing. His father was always a phone call away, but that phone call rarely occurred. And when it did happen, it was asking for some financial help, which Antoine or his mother couldn't afford.

As Antoine aged, he was expected to help out with his expenses such as clothes and food. He got a job at the early age of 14 just so he could afford to buy shoes at Goodwill and the occasional treat at the neighborhood 7-Eleven. His mom was a manager of a fast food restaurant where she worked double shifts to cover her "habit." She ate her meals there and occasionally brought Antoine home some leftovers. Most months, she had trouble covering the rent on the efficiency apartment they shared together but managed to avoid eviction. He didn't see a lot of her which was just as well. He enjoyed his space and Antoine grew independent. He knew the only person he could rely upon was himself.

As Antoine grew older, he grew less and less sympathetic to those who were having financial struggles. He got out of his miserable household slaving away at his side jobs during his younger years and managed to do well in high school to achieve a full-ride scholarship at a local community college. He expected others to just pull themselves up by their bootstraps just like he did.

Present day: Antoine is college-educated and has a respectable job with good pay and benefits as an electrical engineer with a financially solid company. He doesn't think he has OCD, but aspects of his personality would give the impression of being obsessive compulsive. For example, his closet was color coordinated, with identical hangers all facing the same way.

His apartment was spotless. If a single item were crooked or out of place, Antoine would go ape-shit.

That being said, Antoine was happy. He still had contact with his mother in his mature years, and she got better with age as well, kicking her gambling habit. He became friends in adulthood.

Let's go back to Antoine's pet peeve. He absolutely hated when things were out of place, mislabeled, or misdescribed. The thing that irked him the most was the butchering of his given name. He invariably would spell it out when leaving a voicemail and even when meeting someone for the first time. The only thing he had received from his father was his name, and he was proud of it.

Antoine got his morning cup of joe just like millions of Americans, but there was something that totally enraged him. He once got his morning latte, and the barista asked for his name. "Antoine," he would say carefully spelling it out and explaining the pronunciation. Inevitably, when the barista called out his name, it was butchered.

The barista would announce: "Latte for An-ton." When there was no response, she'd try again: Latte for Antone!" Antoine would just smile and take his latte, secretly envisioning an excruciatingly painful death for the barista.

One time the barista asked how to spell it despite the fact that he usually did so and had been coming there for most work days for the last three months. Antione said, "Antoine as in

Ant-wahn." Well, the fucking barista spelled it on the cup "Ant-Yawn." At least this time she said his name correctly.

After this latest fuckup, Antoine was furious. No more

Tonys. No more Antons. No more being called Ant. His name was Antoine, and he was determined that no barista would ever fuck up his name again. So he did what any reasonable, sane person would do. He let it go... for the time being. He assumed that his name was just one of those things in life that were out of his control.

Then one day, Antoine and a coworker were discussing the annoying habits of underlings after a brutal team meeting, and he heard about Mindefusement. "This company looks legit," his friend said, sharing the website on his laptop. "They can film your fantasy for what looks like a reasonable price."

Antoine didn't hesitate. He had some money saved, and didn't figure his movie would cost all that much. He eagerly paid the deposit and was hooked up with veteran pre-screener Jake.

"This is my first time, so you'll probably have to spoon feed me through this on what to expect," Antoine said.

"No problem," Jake said. "This is the pre-screening, and if you are a viable candidate, we'll be giving you a welcome package ASAP."

"Great!" Antoine said, flustered since he expected this would take some time.

"So what do you have in mind?" asked Jake.

"Well, I kinda need your help, having never done this before. Like, what kinda stuff do you do?"

"Everything," Jake enthusiastically recited, "Mutilations, murders, dismemberment, torture... you name it. We do, however, avoid rape scenes as that's not the CEO's cup of tea."

"Well, I don't want to kill somebody. Maybe maim or severely injure a barista?"

"Over what?"

"Mis-pronouncing my fuckin' name. I hate it."

"And your name is... Antoine?" Jake asked trying desperately to remember how it was pronounced. Jake was very concerned that Antoine might want to make fantasy a reality if he fucked it up.

"You understand that this is fantasy violence, correct?" Jake asked phrasing carefully.

"Yeah, like, fuck, I don't want to hurt anybody for real if you know what I'm saying."

Jake understood, gave an inaudible sigh of relief, and continued, "So we have these things we call torture templates. We film them for the clients, such as yourself, and then you can watch it as many times as you like for your amusement."

"Or maybe give it to the fucking barista that screws up my name, am I right?"

"Well, we prefer clients to keep the torture templates to themselves. Due to some legal mumbo-jumbo, the movies are the property of Mindefusement, but you are allowed private viewing when the film is completed. You open yourself up to liability if the movie is shared with others."

"That's fine," Antoine replied without hesitation. Antoine continued, "I want to see the barista write my name on a chalkboard ten-thousand fucking times. Learn to say it. Learn to embrace it. Learn to love my name just as much as me. Know no word but fucking Antoine."

"And then?" Jake asked.

"I dunno. Toss the dude from a fucking building and watch that dumb ass explode like a watermelon on the street below. And then all the splatter matter just happens to spell out Antoine correctly."

"That would be quite epic," Jake said surprised and unable to hold back a laugh.

"And then everybody would be celebrating me. Like I was the king. Because baristas have gotten the message that it's no longer cool to fuck with someone's name like that."

"Damn right," Jake said trying to relate to the client's frustration.

"The cops would come up to me and try to arrest me and shit. And I'd be all, look, I'm a hero. Everyone is congratulating me on striking a blow for freedom against idiotic baristas. Then the cops would be like, hey yeah! Now we can get our coffee and not have our names fucked up too."

Jake smiled. "That sounds like an exciting and imaginative torture template, Antoine. I'm sure one of our directors would love to film it. So, are you ready to proceed to the next step? Do you want to become a Mindefusement client?"

"Yeah, I'd love to see that in action, so yes, count me in."

"Okay, in just a few moments you'll have someone at your door with our welcome package. It was very nice talking with you today, Antoine." Jake made damned sure he pronounced the name correctly.

"Wow! Sounds good, Jake. And thanks for mostly not fucking up my name."

Jake laughed, "No promises in the future, okay?"

Antoine chuckled and hung up from the call. His doorbell rang shortly thereafter with Amanda delivering the package.

Chapter 11
REPUTATION DESTRUCTION

It was only a few weeks after Julie's thorough presentation on the legality of Mindefusement when Jason got the idea that Mindefusement could take on more clientele if they pursued reputation destruction. See, some clients didn't just want a fantasy. A lot of those who contacted Mindefusement wanted revenge against someone to happen in real life rather than a surrogate actor or actress set against a blue screen.

Jason pondered this scenario, and with some research from outside consultants, he came up with a way to destroy reputations in such a way that was harmless enough not to draw any attention to the company. He concluded that ruining someone's reputation was insanely easy.

Jason slaved away on his PowerPoint presentation. The CEO agreed to a private meeting in his giant corner office, which was outfitted with a projector for Jason to use for his presentation.

Jason invited some new faces. Eric, an outside security consultant, was present. The CEO, Jake, and two contractors were in the meeting. The contractors were ex-F.B.I. or equivalent. Julie was absent from the meeting because Jason didn't want her there voicing her opinion on the new product line he was proposing.

Jason began his presentation. His first slide was a picture of a brain with an eye-dropper inserted. The rest of the room gasp and looked at Jason for an explanation.

"Today I'm going to talk about reputation destruction. This is just a brainstorming exercise about a possible new venture that Mindefusement could take on," Jason explained.

Jason flipped to the next slide that showed Mindefusement's profit-and-loss statement he graciously received from accounting. "So we're making a decent profit on these movies," Jason stated. "But what if we could make more?"

Jake, the sales guy, piped up, "We do have some clients who do want to pursue some reputation destruction. We only pass about forty-percent of our pre-screening clients to work with Mindefusement because the majority of our contacts really want something to happen to a specific person rather than simply get vicarious pleasure from seeing him physically tortured in a film. And we have the added cost of sending the on-site pre-screeners to the client's physical location."

"So we need another service to cover all our clientele

and improve our profit margins," Jason stated.

Eric, the security consultant, added confidently, "Destroying reputations is easy and doesn't require the time or expense of finding suitable doubles, costly sets, CGI, or hiring a director. Oh, and there are so many easy ways of doing this. If we get into this business, I guarantee you won't be disappointed with your profits."

Jason flipped to his next slide which was about data gathering. "So it's pretty easy to get a credit card number for those whose reputations are to be destroyed. Eric, you know a little about that. How about you explain?"

"Okay," Eric said, "If we know who is the issuer of the credit card, we already know the first six numbers of the card."

The room sat silent with this new knowledge.

Eric continued, "And if they throw away a receipt, or receive a paper statement, which we can steal from their mailbox or otherwise intercept, we can get their last four digits. Then we have six numbers left to guess. I can use a special script for the remaining numbers that will authenticate with Visa and Mastercard to make sure it's a valid card without doing a charge. So then we have the full credit card number."

Jake's ears perked up, "And then?"

"We can subscribe them to questionable magazines, sign them up for child porn, etc."

Jake responded, "And how will this not get back to us?"

"We can sell the credit card number on the darknet and have someone else do the bidding," Eric responded.

As Eric finished his sentence, Julie walked by the

CEO's office to deliver a memo to him, and politely knocked on the door, opened it a crack, and peeked in. She saw the mass of people and the PowerPoint. "What's going on?" she asked.

Jason replied, "We're talking about a lucrative new product for Mindefusement: reputation destruction."

Julie's face flushed as her temper rose to the boiling point in nanoseconds. Keeping her voice low and even she said, "Did you not understand my presentation a few weeks ago on how to remain within the bounds of legality for the company? And now you're advocating a new product that will include tortious and probably criminal actions affecting the lives of real people?! Reputation destruction is illegal all the way, and I demand as legal counsel that this meeting be adjourned immediately!"

Jason scoffed at Julie, "See this is why I didn't invite you to the meeting."

Julie barked back, "And don't you ever go behind my back again like this you fucking asshole."

The CEO responded, trying to calm both parties down, "Let's at least hear what he has to say. Julie, have a seat and listen to the proposal."

Julie grabbed a chair and sat down, still simmering at the absurdity of the company opening a product line for destroying someone's reputation without realizing the obvious liability it would incur.

Jason, ignoring Julie's hostile stare, asked, "So we can get their credit card number easily?"

Eric replied, "So easy. We can even set up a fake wi-fi network and get more information. Most computers are promiscuous with their networks, and if you set up an insecure one, we can track pretty much all of their network activity including passwords and what not."

"This is completely illegal." Julie again stated. "There is no way I can conceive of a way to 'bless' this endeavor from a legal much less a moral perspective. I don't see how a man like you, Mr. Shiner, can be okay with even the idea Jason is proposing."

The CEO said, "I'm not for this, Julie. I just want to hear what Jason has to say."

"Understood," Jason stated realizing he was facing imposing opposition. "This is just a brainstorming session. We're not going to go forward with this. I'm just putting together a proposal."

"Then why waste the time of the CEO, employees, and contractors by having a meeting with this ridiculous proposal rather than circulating a brief memo?" Julie asked pointedly.

Jason, ignoring Julie's question, continued, "Let me flip to the next slide. This one is called SS7. It allows us to spoof a cell tower and have the user connect to us."

Eric replied, "Yeah, it allows us to intercept all cell traffic, including the person we want to destroy. We can even pretend to be that person and send calls and texts as that person."

"This is insane!" Julie yelled.

Jason replied, "Exactly. So we can do a combination of ruining credit and also identity theft."

The ex-F.B.I. guy said, "Yeah, we called this Stingray when I was with the bureau. We used it to track drug dealers who thought they were smart with changing phones and such. It wasn't hard to find them. It takes five seconds."

"Since Mindefusement is not a legal criminal investigative agency like the FBI, what other illegal things are you suggesting we do?" Julie asked, sarcastically.

"We can fuck with their GPS," Eric said. "We can send them to remote places or wherever the hell we want. We can send them to places that are forbidden to them, such as drug houses, schools if you're a sex offender, and place you in locations where they might have a restraining order. And if we know their name and birth date, which is easy to get if you tip the bartender enough, we can see their voter registration and party affiliation. Even change their registration."

"Okay, I've heard enough," Julie said, getting up from her chair in the CEO's office and heading to the door. Julie turned and said: "Just know that I will be forced to submit my resignation if you go through with this, Mr. Shiner."

The CEO responded, "Julie, you're saying all of this is illegal?"

Julie turned again and exclaimed, "Hell yes, this is illegal! Why are we evenly contemplating doing this?!"

Jason responded, "Because it pays well. And again, this is just a brainstorming session."

"Well, if it ever comes back to us, Mindefusement is well and truly fucked. You'll all need lawyers and are destined to end up in prison on federal charges. And you won't do well in prison, Jason, you future ass fuckee."

The ex-F.B.I. guy responded to Julie, "It won't get back

to us. We're ghosts. The person won't know what hit them."

"You better hope that's true. After all, you're ex-F.B.I., and there are a lot more people in prison that want more than your ass." Julie remarked as she exited the room in disgust.

Jason flipped to the last slide.

"I expect reputation destruction to be priced starting in the $5,000 range. It's a bit much, but our clients are already used to a deposit to work with us, and it's the equivalent of what you'd pay on the darknet."

The CEO decided, "Let's keep this on the back burner. Maybe Jake will come across a good case where we can put this to use."

Jason replied, "But we don't have the blessing of legal."

"I'll deal with Julie," the CEO said.

Jason smiled, "Then let's keep our eyes and ears open."

Chapter 12
RENEE

R enee Shiner, George Shiner's daughter, was your typical struggling college student living in a dormitory in upper Manhattan. Luckily her affiliation with Richard Shiner, her demonic brother, didn't come back to bite her in her studies. She was attending University nearby concentrating on getting a drama degree which her father wasn't totally in approval of. He agreed to pay her tuition hoping she would come to her senses and pursue a career that was more remunerative, but she was on her own otherwise.

Renee was moderately attractive, with auburn hair and what some would call a skinny figure, similar to comedian Michelle Wolfe. She wasn't confident enough to go out for any auditions, so she concentrated well on her studies.

Renee had a stalker situation. Her stalker situation

started with what normal humans call a favor. Renee, a desperate college student in need, frequented her favorite Keggles for groceries. Marc, the general manager of the small mom-and-pop store type in Manhattan noticed her and was very attracted.

Marc, being the fake nice guy he was, saw a young helpless female in desperate need of a job since every time she came in she whined about the cost of the groceries. Marc asked if she would be up for a job doing the accounting, inventory, and occasional cashiering over her summer break. She would even get an employee discount. Renee enthusiastically agreed, and Marc's inner-boner became rock hard at the acceptance of his offer. She was already in his clutches as far as he was concerned.

Renee was oblivious to the nature of Marc's dirty crush, even though Marc's girlfriend was already basking in his attention. Marc inwardly thought that maybe they'd want a three-some sometime; he'd just have to work up to it.

Renee, not taking classes at the University for summer, desperately needed the job, so she took it on with force. Her work ethic was so great that she finished ahead of schedule, especially with the easy stuff like managing inventory. She loved every aspect of the job.

She did notice, however, that Marc wanted to get inside her bubble at times. He would always rub her on the shoulder lightly whenever possible or touch her "accidentally." She would politely smile back, but while uncomfortable, really did not fear Marc or anything.

The cause of conflict came from Mario, with whom Renee was communicating with on Instagram. She had developed romantic feelings for Mario, and then Mario announced he was coming to visit her in New York. She was elated at the news. Renee could barely wait for Mario's arrival.

Renee asked for time off, and Marc grudgingly gave it. He knew she was up to something because he had been following her on Instagram and noticed increased activity and interaction with Mario.

While on vacation spending every minute with Mario, Renee showed him the sights around Manhattan and other tourist spots around New York City. Renee began to believe her feelings for Mario were perhaps love. But things quickly turned sour when she returned to work.

"So how are things with Mario?" Marc scoffed at her. He explained, "Long distance never works."

She was a more than a bit weirded out by his comments since she'd never mentioned Mario to him, She realized he had been following her Instagram account. At that point, she remembered Marc's vague efforts to ask her out or visit her. She also remembered Marc's sexual references such as his joke, "Well, you'd get a bonus for a threesome." She did the books: she knew there was no bonus.

Fast forward to University starting up again, and she quit her job with adequate notice. Marc continually tried to message her on Instagram. She would politely respond occasionally.

The kicker here is Mario. He decided he loved Renee and asked her to marry him. She agreed with an unconditional "yes." Mario decided to permanently move to Manhattan to be near his fiancée.

Marc's obsession and stalking Renee went into over-drive. He tried to visit Renee at her dormitory, but she told security to tell him she was out or in class if he happened to visit. His Instagram stalking also evolved into setting up multiple accounts and trying to message both Mario and Renee. He would even set up fake numbers and try to message her.

It seemed nothing would stop Marc, and separation made his obsession for Renee grow stronger as his fantasy of a life with her blossomed. Marc even broke up with his girlfriend and Instagrammed Renee saying he was single and ready to be with her. Renee was appalled and repelled by the increased level of attention and was just overwhelmed.

Renee knew she needed to take action. Before getting a victim protection order, she called her friend at Mindefusement, Cassandra, with whom she had gone to high school. Cassandra was sympathetic to the situation and suggested she talk to Jake and gave her his number. The goal was to prevent Marc from stalking Renee as well as others who might be victims to his incessant nagging.

Renee's call with Jake was short. She wanted real-life intervention to get Marc out of her life. Jake said that Mindefusement did not do real-life interventions, but would pass the case over to Jason, as he had some ideas on how to destroy reputations.

Jason received the request and was surprised and delighted to learn Renee was the CEO's daughter. He had been chomping at the bit to try out reputation destruction, and this seemed like the perfect test case. Jason hurried to Jake's office to discuss the case with him.

"Can I talk to you about Renee?" Jason asked.

Jake replied, "Yes, I talked to her briefly, but nothing came of it. I figure you can take it from here if you want."

Jason replied, "I don't have the means. I haven't gotten much buy-in from anybody around here considering it's not really legal to destroy reputations."

"It may be illegal," Jake thought out loud, "But we can use her as a test case, and if we succeed, Mr. Shiner will be impressed." Jake inwardly salivated at the idea of showing the CEO how useful, necessary, and lucrative this new product could be and imagined his increased commissions.

Jake decided to set up a pre-screening call with Renee as per protocol. Jake explained Mindefusement filmed client's fantasies as a means to provide closure. Renee burst into tears. Weeping, she explained the stalker situation and how it was escalating, and while her father hadn't told her the inner-workings of Mindefusement, there was no way a "fantasy film" was going to take care of the problem. Jake said he would get back to her.

Jake walked back into Jason's office and said, "I just pre-screened Renee. I think she would be a perfect client for in your reputation destruction operations. If we succeed with this and show how effective the product can be, I think we can impress the CEO in spite of legal's objection. Can you set that up?"

Without hesitation, Jason replied, "You betcha! What are the details?"

"Well, Renee has a bad stalker situation," Jake said. Jake replayed in his mind the video call with Renee and said, "I think we can help her out here with the right resources. She's in Manhattan, so I know things can get expensive there."

"Oooof. You're right." Jason cringed knowing that setting up an operation in Manhattan would be pricey.

"What does your gut tell you, Jake? Should we help her?" Jason inquired.

"I think that we, as a company, can really help the client and should. Whether it's legal or not, this stalker needs to be stopped."

After talking to Jake, they decided to try out reputation destruction without either the knowledge or approval of the CEO or Julie. They knew they had absolutely no chance of getting a green light for the new product unless they could prove its value.

Jason suggested, "We could start with muscle. Ya know, have somebody 'talk' to the stalker? That wouldn't cost much."

"What do you mean by 'talk'"? Jake asked.

"I'm suggesting we hire a couple of bouncers to approach Marc after work," Jason replied thinking out loud.

"That sounds good. What happens if he isn't dissuaded and keeps it up?" asked Jake.

"We'll take more drastic measures, like Samuel L. Jackson in Pulp Fiction. Like really destroying his reputation so that stalking our client is the last thing on his mind."

"So how much do you think all of this is going to cost?'

"At least two thousand for the bouncers. More if we have to go there in person. Can she afford that?"

Jason asked.

"No, she's a broke ass college student and not employed. She asked to make payments over time."

"Wow! That's no good." Jason exclaimed. "We're not a bank."

Jake proposed, "How about we use this as a proof-of-concept?"

"As in, we take this case on a pro-bono basis?" Jason asked.

"Exactly," Jake replied.

After a few moments of thought by Jason, he finally replied, "Let's do it!"

"Roger that." Jake agreed. "I'll send over the details of the stalker. He shouldn't be hard to find given the information we have."

"Yep, most people are not hard to find at all," Jason smirked.

Jake immediately called Renee and informed her of the situation. He explained that they were willing to deal with her case for free due to her financial situation.

Renee was overwhelmed with gratitude and effusively thanked Jake. "But what are you going to do to stop Marc?" Renee asked.

"We're having internal discussions about our options which you really don't need or want to know. But consider the problem with him taken care of. We'll have something set up within a week or two, but do not communicate with this asshole, okay?"

Renee agreed enthusiastically and replied, "Thank You!"

Jake gave a southern, "You're mighty welcome

little lady!" and hung up. Jake felt proud of his work at Mindefusement that day.

Chapter 13

MARC

Jason did the research on Marc and learned he had been the manager of Keggles for a better part of ten years. This wasn't Marc's first harassment complaint, but the company trusted Marc's word and stood behind him.

It took Jake and Jason two weeks to find a couple of discreet bouncers to go have a talk with Marc. As Jake and Jason discussed, it would be best to have a "talk" with Marc before things escalated. The bouncers they hired to talk to Marc had more interest in action rather than just talking, however.

Jason and Jake pumped a couple of grand of Mindefusement's money into this and attempted to cover-up with another client for accounting. In reality, it wasn't a possible sales venture and instead the money was to cover two New York City bouncers.

The bouncers patiently waited in a nondescript vehicle across from the Keggles. They waited until Marc had closed the Keggles for the night. When Marc left the store, the bouncers exited the vehicle and approached him as he turned the final key in the latch closing the store. Marc pulled down the overhead metal screen for the store and locked it. Each bouncer grabbed one of Marc's arms and propelled him into a nearby alley, with Marc screaming and struggling all the way. There were a few bystanders who witnessed this altercation, but none of them cared to call the police or help.

"Get the fuck off of me!" Marc demanded. An elbow to his nose was given in response, causing blood to gush from his nose. The bouncers continued to drag Marc into the alley and pushed him up against the store's dumpster face-first, breaking his glasses. Turning him around, one of the bouncers pinned him to the dumpster, holding his shoulders in a firm grip. The bouncer had a hundred pounds of pure muscle over Marc's one hundred and sixty-pound non-athletic physique. Marc's frantic but useless attempt to escape was like a small mouse trying to escape a cat's clutches.

"Do you know this girl?" One of the bouncers asked Marc as he shoved a picture of Renee under Marc's nose. Marc looked at it through his now broken glasses, with blood soaking his shirt and tie due to his broken nose.

The smell of blood quickly overpowered Marc's senses. He was in excruciating pain from the blow to his face. "No!" Marc screamed. The other bouncer sent a well-placed kick to Marc's stomach. Marc began to throw up after the blow.

The bouncer argued, "You know her. Her name is Renee. Admit it or I'll kick you again, but even harder."

Marc's silence was met with additional violence. The other bouncer delivered a punch to his rib cage, breaking two of Marc's ribs, followed by a hard uppercut to Marc's jaw, breaking a couple of teeth.

Marc, reeling in agony finally was able to speak and admitted, "Yes, yes, I know her!"

The second bouncer held the picture close. "You are not to talk to her. Visit her. Go anywhere near her. Or we will fuck you up way worse than tonight. Understood?"

Marc groaned from the pain in his rib cage. "Okay, no more Renee."

The second bounder swept his legs, dropping him to the filthy alley pavement. Marc was in too much pain to get up.

"Renee is out of your vocabulary now. You even think about her and I'll dick punch you so hard you'll be tasting your cock through your mouth as it enters your throat."

It started raining. The alley was slippery with both the rain and Marc's blood. He struggled to get up, but couldn't. He talked through the pain, "I won't fuck with Renee again. I'm sorry."

Both bouncers, satisfied, gave Marc a final kick and left him alone to soak in the cold rain next to the smelly dumpster in the alleyway.

"We'll do you a favor and call 911. It looks like you're not getting up," one of the bouncers joked. Marc still had his phone. He could call 911 by himself, which he planned to do once the bouncers finally left.

The bouncers gave each other a fist bump as they returned to their vehicle. Marc heard them laughing as they slammed the doors, started the motor, and drove off.

One of the bouncers picked up his phone and called Jason's mobile. The bouncer announced, "Marc's out of the picture for now with a lengthy recovery time and dental work needed. Tell Renee she can relax."

Jason replied, "You were supposed to just talk."

The bouncer laughed, "We don't like to talk." The bouncer laughed and then hung up.

And just like that, the stalking stopped... for about a month. Apparently, the hospital visit that night after the confrontation only temporarily dampened Marc's fixation on Renee. Marc wrote Renee a long letter asking why she would resort to such drastic measures. He hounded her to let him visit her in the dormitory to talk and constantly tracked Renee on multiple Instagram accounts to get an answer.

Renee contacted Jake at Mindefusement and told him Marc was stalking her again with renewed energy. Jake and Jason met and decided it was time for reputation destruction to be launched.

Fast forward a few weeks, and there was a white panel van with a large array of antennas on top parked right outside Keggles. Jason wanted to go on this field trip to see reputation destruction first-hand and hired a technology expert to set up a fake cell network. The technician began fiddling with the equipment inside the van.

"What are you doing?" Jason asked the technician

inside the van.

"I'm setting up a fake cell network. I hope Marc's phone connects to it, as well as some others." the technician replied.

"And then?" Jason asked.

"With luck, Marc's phone will switch over to our cell signal. Just watch and learn. You're distracting me," the technician said irritably.

Several minutes went by, and the technician clapped his hands. "Yes! We got him! As well as 200 others."

"200 others are connected to our fake cell tower?"

"Yup," the technician said, smiling.

"So, what are you going to do next?" Jason replied.

The technician, becoming ever more annoyed with Jason's questions, asked him to be quiet. Jason passed several moments in uncomfortable silence as he waited for the technician to respond. Jason's impatience got the better of him. "Are we going to do this?" Jason grumbled in frustration breaking the silence.

"Yep. Now let's ruin his reputation." the technician finally replied.

The technician began typing, "Dear Patron. Marc, the manager at Keggles, is a stalker, and he won't leave an innocent girl alone. Please tell him to stop."

"What's that?" Jason asked.

"A text from Marc's cell phone to the 200 other people we have on the same tower."

"So 200 people around Marc are going to receive this message?"

"Yep, from even Marc himself. That's the magic." the

technician began laughing.

"Wow. This will really crush him." Jason said concerned.

"I just do what I'm paid to do. And from the looks of it, it was you who paid me," the technician smiled.

"So what now? Send?" Jason questioned.

The crowd around Keggles were observed checking their phones at the incoming text message.

"I just sent the text, and you can see the confused looks on people's faces in the grocery store already." Jason saw the people in and around Keggles check their phones and immediately look around for Marc.

"Yep," Jason replied.

"Those customers just realized they shop with a creeper." the technician explained.

Jason watched as several patrons of Keggles approached Marc and a screaming match ensued. Those outside on the sidewalk just looked towards the store in disgust. Marc's reputation and career were done for.

In fact, Marc's life and livelihood were over. You see, some millennial with too much time on her hands recorded the engagement between the customers and Marc. Marc tried defending himself, but the customers weren't having it. The video recording ended up having over two million views with it being shared publicly on Facebook. Apparently, people love the story of a man-stalker getting his karma.

In the case of Mindefusement, their job with Marc was done. Renee was a happy client and agreed to pay back Mindefusement in full a couple of hundred dollars a month or more quickly if she got a job acting. Renee could go on with her life and her engagement in peace, while Jason and Jake now had proved their concept was viable.

Jake and Jason realized that what they did was illegal. Ignoring the overly zealous bouncers who went far beyond the instructions given, the fact that they set up a fake cell network was damningly illegal. A cover-up began with accounting, as they knew the CEO and Julie would review the books. Accounting wanted an explanation for a ten-thousand-dollar line item. Jake, trying to help cover up for Jason, explained that the New York trip was for the purpose of enhancing company security.

Jake lied adding, "I ended up getting several new clients."

Other than receipts for travel and a motel room, Jason had nothing to back up his "miscellaneous" expenses. The accounting department easily saw through the scheme, and wasn't buying any of it, including Jake's justification to increase business. The chief accountant replied, "You're going to have to take this up with the CEO with detailed receipts on how the money was spent and provide names of clients who signed up as result of Jason's trip."

Jake was dismayed. He had no receipts and no new clients. He knew he'd have to come clean to the CEO. But regardless, he felt good about what he helped do to Marc. Accounting reported the transaction to the CEO, and the CEO called Jake into his office.

To say the CEO was less than cordial with Jake is a vast understatement. As soon as Jake entered the office, Mr. Shiner lit into him, verbally ripping him a new one. "What in the hell did you spend over ten thousand on in

New York?!" yelled the CEO in a murderous rage.

Jake came clean immediately, "Jason and I pursued a reputation destruction use-case with a lady named Renee. We hired a couple of muscle men to talk to the cretin, and when that didn't work, we hacked his cellular network."

"You did what?!" the CEO exclaimed. "Julie made it clear that absolutely nothing about your concept for reputation destruction was legal. You and Jason are history!"

The CEO hesitated and asked, "Renee who?"

Jake replied, "She's your daughter, sir. So I thought it would be okay to use her as a test case."

"Oh, I should fire your asses immediately. Using my daughter? How the fuck dare you involve my daughter!"

Jake met the CEO's glare and replied: "I fully understand your position, however, even losing my job is worth it. We were able to stop a stalker from making a young girl's life a living hell. She just happened to be your daughter."

"How did she contact you?" the CEO growled.

"Through Cassandra, our support rep that she went to high school with. She gave her my number."

The CEO fumed silently while he digested this information. He wasn't aware of Renee's stalker situation and wondered why she hadn't come to him for help. He regretted that his decision in opposing her chosen career path had put a wall between them. If Renee had just confided in her father, he could've taken care of the situation legally.

After a prolonged silence during which Mr. Shiner wrestled with his emotions for his daughter and her suffering, and his anger with his employees going behind his back, he sighed inwardly and stated sternly: "You and Jason are valuable assets of Mindefusement. However, both of you are on probationary status. Neither of you are to take a shit without me knowing about it! Both of you better hope nobody ever links your actions to Mindefusement. If there is even a hint that Mindefusement was involved, you will be fired and turned over to the legal authorities for prosecution. I'll have to inform Julie about everything that happened, and I imagine she'll demand you and Jason be terminated immediately. Lawyers hate cover-ups, so you and Jason need to write up what happened leaving nothing out. You're dismissed. I suggest you and Jason stay out of my sight and keep a low profile."

Jake nodded and left the CEO's office. Regardless of the trouble he was in, he felt he had done the right thing. He had a smile on his face for the first time in a long while on his drive home from work.

As for Marc: he was summarily fired from Keggles, went home, and committed suicide.

Chapter 14

THE FALLOUT

M r. Shiner summoned his general counsel to his office the morning after his confrontation with Jake and gave Julie the abridged version of Jake's and Jason's reputation destruction of Marc. To say Julie was infuriated was an understatement. "You need to get those two in here immediately! I need to know every single detail to protect the company from the fallout which is bound to hit, and the sooner I know what we're facing in the way of liability, the better!"

The CEO summoned Jake and Jason to his office as requested. Doing her best to keep her temper in check, Julie began: "Before we get into the details, I want to know why you two went forward with a proposal that had been rejected outright? I'm also wondering why you two still have jobs," shifting her attention to the CEO.

Jason and Jake were silent, staring at the plush carpet. Focusing on Jason, Julie continued, "Remember when I warned you not to dare go behind my back?"

Jason with eyes still downcast started to reply, "Yes, but ..."

Julie interrupted, "Well, you really fucked things up royally. You realize the guy's whose reputation you destroyed is dead?"

Marc's suicide was fresh news for Jake and Jason, and they looked at each other in confusion before turning toward Julie.

"How did he die?" Jake asked.

"Oh, so now you fucking give a shit?" Julie responded sharply.

Jake, flabbergasted, replied, "Yes, I'd like to know."

"He committed suicide after you morons destroyed his reputation and got him fired from his job."

"In what fashion?" Jason asked.

"Un-fucking-believable! You don't give a rat's ass that he's dead, but want to know the sordid details?" Julie responded in indignation.

"Yes, I'd like to know."

The CEO interrupted Julie's tirade against Jason and Jake and matter-of-factly stated: "He used an electrical cord tied to the ceiling fan and stood on a stool. He took an entire bottle of Ambien. When the Ambien kicked in, he went limp, and gravity took care of the rest."

The room was silent as Jason and Jake digested this information.

"In other words, the actions of you two idiots are

responsible for Marc's death. You killed him. And if this… rather when this gets back to Mindefusement, we will not and cannot protect you." Julie replied. She continued, "Now I want to know the exact details of what happened."

Jake replied, "Well, Jason was on-point for that one, but I know what happened."

"And?" Julie pressed.

"We hired a couple of local bouncers to talk to Marc and to tell him to stop stalking Renee. The bouncers weren't really into talking, however. They beat the shit out of him, and he ended up in the hospital."

Jason chimed in, "But that didn't stop him. Once he was back on his feet, he continued to stalk Renee within a month after the beat down by the bouncers. So, we decided it was time to test out reputation destruction to take him down by giving Marc something else to focus on instead of harassing a young college student."

"Very noble of you," said Julie, her voice dripping with sarcasm. "What did you do?"

"We used a fake cell tower to send out a text to tell people he is a creeper."

Julie, almost screaming, replied, "Totally illegal! Not to mention soliciting the bouncers! You two better look for a good lawyer to represent you because Mindefusement did not sanction this. You'll be facing both state and federal charges."

Julie, turned back to the CEO and asked, "And why are these two cretins still employed by the company?"

The CEO took a deep breath before he replied, "Renee is my daughter. Obviously, I have some sympathy for what

Jake and Jason did to help her."

"Well, your sympathy is misplaced. It will lead to your downfall and the end of Mindefusement," Julie threatened.

"I don't think it will get back to us," Jason replied. "Did Marc leave any kind of note when he committed suicide?"

"As far as I can tell, no," Julie responded. "The cause for his suicide was pretty self-evident... fired from his job, his reputation completely destroyed, etc."

Jake smiled, "So why do we need lawyers or have any worries at this point? I see this as a douche bag being outed for stalking that no one will care about."

"The likelihood of this eventually coming back to Mindefusement is completely foreseeable for anyone who wants to follow the dots. First, Marc is beaten to a pulp after locking up and hospitalized. Shortly after the assault, his cell phone is hacked and hundreds of people who don't know Marc at all who happen to be in the neighborhood of Keggles are notified that he is a stalker. Marc's stalking victim, Renee, is the CEO's daughter. Someone is going to dig into Marc's suicide. The connection is there for anyone who is interested."

Julie continued, "And I want to reiterate my position: if the company chooses to pursue reputation destruction as a new product, I will be forced to hand in my resignation should it continue as soon as I exit this office."

"Renee was a special case with emotional ties to our company," Jake replied. "While it took care of her problem, I agree the risk of using reputation destruction outweighs the benefits to other clients and the bottom-line for the company. Marc's suicide was an unfortunate, unforeseeable consequence."

"I would hope the jury would see it that way," Julie said dryly. "Marc was a douche. Did he deserve to die? No. Will it come back to fuck us? Probably. But you're the one who will be in the line of fire, Jake. You and Jason did this by pilfering Mindefusement funds and going against the Mindefusement mission."

The CEO spoke, "While I didn't authorize it, It was a good first case study even if the person being stalked had not been a member of my family. But I want reputation destruction to cease immediately. And the fact you used Mindefusement funds? That's a fireable offense. You two are both lucky to still have your jobs."

Julie responded to the CEO, "I can't continue with this company with these two still employed. They need to be turned over to the authorities for their actions in hiring the bouncers regardless of the fact that the bouncers went beyond what they were asked to do. They also broke any number of federal and state laws by hacking Marc's phone, not to mention a cell tower and network. If you aren't willing to follow my legal advice, I have no option but to resign immediately."

The CEO wasn't used to having his decisions questioned. He replied sharply, "If you resign, the arrangements we made for your brother will be terminated immediately. You will be unemployable just as you were before we hired you, and both you and he will be out on the street. Think about that before making a snap decision!"

"How dare you br…"Julie said before being interrupted.

"Your brother's protection was a perk of your employment. If you are no longer an employee, that perk is no longer available." the CEO said.

Julie paused to collect her thoughts. She knew she could survive, but had concerns about Stuart. Finally, she replied: "Fine. This is blackmail, but I'll ride this out and see where it goes for my brother's sake."

Jason said, changing the topic back, "I appreciate your objectivity and sincerity, Mr. Shiner. And no more thoughts of reputation destruction will cross my mind again. Ever. You have my word."

Julie scoffed, "I wish 'your word' meant shit. Just do your job in idiocy like you always do. Stay the fuck away from anybody who EVER wants to do something for real at Mindefusement. And Jake… why, would you agree to do this? Did you possibly think this would increase sales? Your search for gold has exposed this you and the company to severe liability issues which directly affects whether you will be able to continue to support that wife of yours that you cheat on and the lovers you entertain on the side."

Jake hesitated and replied, "I truly felt reputation destruction would increase the company's sales and its bottom line. In this case, it was too successful. We put the stalker in the hospital, and then, ended up basically killing him."

"So you see where I'm coming from, then?" Julie asked.

"Yes, absolutely. I totally see your point."

Julie paused and said, "So where does that leave us? I despise even the idea of a cover-up, but it's something I've done before as a lawyer. It isn't something I'm proud of doing. But we need some kind of damage control."

The CEO responded, "I'll take care of the accounting issues. We'll give Stella a new video and pass the costs onto her account."

"Ugh!" Julie responded. "Stella is an evil, psychopathic bitch. Why her?"

"Because she's a long-time client of Mindefusement, and it's about time we gave her a break."

"I hope for the sake of Mindefusement and yourself, that you are right, George. I see this coming back to us eventually, even if you manage to cook the books." Julie warned.

"I just want to be clear," the CEO said, "This conversation never happened. We never helped Renee. The idea of reputation destruction was never even remotely considered as a viable service by Mindefusement. We are now and have always been a company providing fantasies to relieve the angst and frustrations of our clients. We never considered, authorized, nor pursued reputation destruction of Marc nor anyone else. None of this happened. And just in case someone leaks this information, I will call Stella myself and after this meeting to have her come up with a torture template to take care of the, uh, accounting problem."

Jason and Jake nodded.

"Do we have your full attention now, Jake and Jason?" Julie asked.

They both responded in the affirmative.

"Good," Julie responded. "So what's next for you two?"

The CEO responded, "Go back and resume normal

work duty. We'll be keeping a close eye on everything you do, from phone calls to how often you go to the bathroom to take a crap. If you ever go behind my or Julie's back again, I don't care if it's my daughter, my locked-up son, or anybody related to Mindefusement, you are out of here. No one is entitled to any special privileges here."

Julie nodded in agreement.

"So are we crystal clear on this, Jake and Jason?" the CEO asked.

"Crystal," Jake replied.

"Yes, crystal clear," Jason said nodding.

"Alright, meeting adjourned." the CEO said firmly.

Julie looked at Jake and Jason in disgust one last time and left the room. The CEO got up and left the room as well.

Jason and Jake, by themselves in Mr. Shiner's opulent office looked at each other in surprise.

"Did we just dodge the bullet?" Jason asked Jake.

"Yep. We're lucky we still have a job. I can't believe Marc killed himself. What a douche."

"Will this come back to us?" Jason asked.

Jake replied, "I doubt it. Don't lose any sleep over this. I believe Marc got what he deserved."

"Me too. Me too." Jason replied.

"Let's go have a couple of drinks. This meeting was intense." Jake suggested.

"Sounds good to me."

Chapter 15

GOING VIRAL

Vanessa stroked her long red hair as she grinned devil-ishly. Her now ex-boyfriend was going to pay. It would be hard for him to ever to get another woman to take him at all.

Having exported her video to Dropbox, she felt the video should go public to dismantle her ex-boyfriend's reputation with the ladies.

Being one of those who exported the video, Jake from Mindefusement called her. "We have new terms of service in the contract that prevents you from sharing any videos publicly. If the video is made public, any liability will be at your own risk. Furthermore, Mindefusement will obtain removal of any public videos through a DCMA request."

Vanessa was less than receptive to the restrictions, as Jake expected. "Look, I already paid for the video. I can do with it what I want," Vanessa told Jake.

"The video is the property of Mindefuseme..." Jake began only to be interrupted.

"Bullshit!" Vanessa replied angrily. She whined, sounding much like a four-year-old whose toy was being taken away, "I am the one who paid for it. It's mine, and I can do what I want with the video!"

Jake, sighing at her resistance responded, "I just want you to fully understand you will be personally liable for any damages caused by the video's public release."

"Understood. Now leave me alone!" Vanessa violently mashed the red receiver button on her phone to disconnect and slammed the phone down in disgust.

Immediately, Vanessa went to her Dropbox account, downloaded the video, and uploaded it to YouTube. "Mindefusement can go to hell." she thought. She posted the video to her Facebook page. Vanessa thought the video was hysterical, and she wanted the world to see it. She knew it would go viral. What she didn't do was send the video to her ex because she didn't want him to report the video and have it shut down before it was widely viewed. She imagined how humiliated he would be when he finally realized why people were laughing and pointing at him, sometimes whispering behind his back.

Then Reddit happened. The video was posted to one of the subreddits and was up-voted as one of the funniest videos ever. Her YouTube views now numbered over one million. She savored all the YouTube and Reddit comments. YouTube declined to honor the DCMA request but did provide a warning that the video contained graphic content.

Mindefusement, however, didn't find the situation amusing at all; they prided themselves as a private and secretive company and a video being shared publicly was on their worst-case scenario list.

Jason was the first to get the news that one of their client's videos was going viral. He was stunned by the number of views and comments, both on the subreddit and on YouTube.

As a result of all of the publicity, applications for pre-screenings for Mindefusement unexpectedly skyrocketed. Jason was overwhelmed with requests. He had to do something, so he interrupted a meeting between the CEO, Jake, and Julie.

Jason, panic-stricken barged into the CEO's office without knocking and blurted out, "We have a disaster on our hands!"

"More serious than what happened with Marc?" Julie asked raising her eyebrows.

"Way more serious," Jason responded.

"Well?" The CEO asked impatiently, "What's the situation?"

"We made it to the top of one of the subreddits when one of our clients posted her torture template video on YouTube."

"Holy shit!" Julie responded.

Jason continued, "The client uploaded the torture template she'd exported from the package to YouTube. Then it went viral on Reddit. It was then eventually shared with her ex."

Julie grumbled loudly, "I told you this shit would come back to bite us! And those redditors don't fuck around! What was the torture template?!"

Jason face-palmed and said, "We call the torture template 'Blue Balls.'" The CEO, Julie, and Jake audibly sucked in their breath, staring at Jason.

He continued, "Some guy who looks like her ex is approached by some hookers and they go back to his hotel room. The girls make out a bit and then undress the man. They start laughing at his penis size and imply that there wouldn't be any scenario in the world where they would fuck him with such a tiny penis. We had the actor wear a blue-screen condom and CGI'd his erect penis size."

Julie, still concerned, smirked, "So it was a humiliation torture template. Clever. But we're still fucked."

"Yeah," Jason replied, agreeing.

Julie exclaimed in frustration, "But it still got back to us via the redditors. They found us quickly because of our introductory logo. That wasn't edited out before publication I'm assuming? I don't see this as good news."

The CEO dryly stated, "It was bound to happen eventually."

"Well," Jason said, "It's been a mixed blessing. A lot of people have been signing up for Mindefusement."

"How many so far?" Jake asked.

"Twenty today," Jason said matter-of-factly.

The room went silent as Jake slowly lost his shit. "Are you fucking kidding me? That's more sign-ups than we usually get in a month! How will I pre-screen twenty fucking people and also have on-site pre-screeners there as well?"

Jason had no good solution, and at that point, nobody in the room had one either.

"What do you suggest, then?" Jason asked blindly.

"Shut down the form. Now!" Jake ordered.

The CEO disagreed and summarized the situation, "So we're so popular now that people are signing up in droves, and we don't have the personnel to handle the load? Is that a correct summary of the problem?"

"Yes," Jake stated, with sweat dripping down his forehead.

The CEO thought for a few moments and then continued, "Let's pull the on-site pre-screener Amanda and have her work the phones. Then we'll mail the package to clients who are approved."

"Remember Lenny? That's the way we used to do it." Jake sharply retorted.

The CEO continued, "We'll increase building security and perhaps hire bodyguards to escort the salespeople home. We already have bodyguards on staff, so that shouldn't be a problem."

Jake thought and responded, "That sounds doable. We'll stop hiring pre-screeners to drop off the package." He continued, "Let's raise the prices. I can probably do 20 pre-screens maybe in a week, but I'm glad that I can rely on Amanda as a pre-screener; she is quite talented."

"And if people continue to sign up?" Jason asked. "I haven't checked in the last thirty minutes. There may be more now."

Jake said, "We'll have to have a waiting list."

The CEO asked, "A waiting list to submit a deposit or a waiting list for people to access the sign-up form?"

Julie, quiet so far, recommended, "Let's make a waiting list for people wanting to sign-up to make a deposit."

"How long will it take for you to program that into our website, Jason?" The CEO asked.

"I can begin working on that immediately," Jason replied.

"Then double the price of the deposit and see if that slows down demand. And add a form so we can collect leads from this waiting list." the CEO concluded.

Jason agreed and quickly exited the CEO's office.

"So Amanda is going to be bumped up to being an in-house pre-screener? She's an awesome on-site pre-screener, but she's going to need some coaching." Jake remarked.

"Fine, you can get busy coaching her. For now. But I'm watching you like a hawk. Remember?" the CEO threatened.

Jake nodded and hustled out of the room to find Amanda to give her the good news about her promotion as he savored the promise of working even more "closely" with her.

Chapter 16

SAMANTHA

S amantha, like Antoine, had a huge pet peeve. She was an avid movie goer and considered herself a movie aficionado. She despised people who interrupted her movies: morons loudly munching popcorn or slurping soft drinks, idiots who brought babies and young children to R-rated movies, and cretins texting on their cell phones. But the ones she despised the most were people who held running conversations giving horrid Michael Bay commentary during the show. She hates Michael Bay because he seems to ruin any movie he directs or produces. So Michael Bay commentary is just anyone ruining the movie for someone else.

Her favorite movie of all time was "American Beauty" directed by Sam Mendes. She loved the symbolism and felt the death scene at the end was a brilliant touch because Lester (one of the characters) finally found his daughter's internal beauty. It's a complicated movie to summarize in a short space, but Lester was going through a troubled marriage and had an almost estranged relationship with his daughter. He felt an infatuation for his daughter's friend and was nearly successful in seducing her. He found his daughter's beauty at the end just before he was shot by an enraged neighbor who was having issues coping with his own sexuality.

Samantha longed for someone to recognize her internal beauty, but nobody seemed to really notice her, not even her boyfriend, Thomas. She didn't want anybody to die before someone recognized her inner beauty, but she often felt like someone had to. Physically, Samantha was truly gorgeous with a curvaceous figure and cute, short brown locks that framed her lovely heart-shaped face.

Thomas, on the other hand, was addicted to his phone and was always staring at it. He would also check out other girls while Samantha only had eyes for him. The relationship was very one-sided. She didn't mind him checking out other girls if it aroused his sexuality so she could finally get laid, even if he was picturing someone else to make him cum.

You're probably wondering why Samantha didn't just dump Thomas and find someone who appreciated her beauty and loyalty. Mainly, it was because of her insecurities that she could not find someone better, and Thomas had an endearing side to him when he wasn't glued to his mobile device. He was addicted to YouTube and other videos online, and he also had a demanding boss who required an instant response to his texts.

She tried taking him to the theater in an effort to bond over their mutual love of comedy and horror, but Thomas was always glued to his mobile and took calls or answered texts in the hallway throughout the movies.

Thomas would also text inside the theater, and it was highly distracting to Samantha and the patrons. During one incident in the theater, the patrons were hostile to Thomas and began throwing Skittles at him. Some of them hit Samantha, and she begged Thomas to get off his phone. They were escorted out of the theater that day due to the theater's strict no cell phone policy.

To say she was furious and embarrassed would be a huge understatement. They argued on the way home and almost broke up over his obsessive cell phone usage. Thomas agreed to not use his cell when they went to future movies. However, Thomas was beyond addicted, so it was an empty promise.

As Samantha's frustration grew with Thomas, she turned to self-help articles on how to repair their strained relationship. She finally came to the conclusion that her boyfriend wasn't going to change without some karma. She, however, didn't want this karma to happen to him in real life. She loved him. After an almost endless amount of searching, she found Mindefusement. She found it through the now-viral video and decided this was perfect for her needs.

She was one of the 20 who signed up with Mindefusement before the waiting list was activated and deposit increased. Amanda, highly capable with on-site pre-screening but new to in-house pre-screening, was given her first solo client call after Jake coached her through a few client calls previously, and Samantha was the client. Through the Google Hangout, Samantha savored Amanda's gorgeous face. On the other end of the Google Hangout, Samantha quickly grew infatuated with Amanda in a way she had never experienced before.

Amanda introduced herself, "Hi, I'm Amanda, your pre-screener."

Flustered, Samantha blurted out, "I'm Samantha. It's so nice to meet you!"

Amanda responded "It's great to meet you, too! Welcome to Mindefusement pre-screening. I just need to get some quick disclaimers out of the way."

"Sure," Samantha said hesitantly.

"Okay, we consider this a pre-screening process. We pre-screen to determine if an individual will make a good Mindefusement client." Amanda continued, "If we don't consider you a good candidate, we will refund your deposit."

"That sounds fine." Samantha agreed.

"Okay, so we have this term called torture templates. Are you familiar with those?"

"No, I'm afraid not."

"Well, consider torture templates to be some fantasy that you wish could be a reality, but they are short films instead."

"Great!" Samantha said enthusiastically.

"As a legal disclaimer, the movies are the property of Mindefusement, but you are allowed private viewing when the film is completed. You may not share the movies with others."

"But that's how I found your company," Samantha said, "Through a Reddit post."

"Ah, the infamous 'Blue Balls' torture template. We are really proud of that, but we didn't agree with the video to go public. As a matter of fact, you'll be signing a contract that prevents any liability to Mindefusement should you share your film with others."

"That's fine," Samantha said after several moments of silence.

"So what do you have in mind?" Amanda asked.

"My boyfriend is addicted to his cell phone. I can't take him anywhere. He even managed to get us both kicked out of a theater. And I was thoroughly enjoying the movie until people started pelting him with Skittles. Some of them hit me, too! I was angry and humiliated!"

Amanda nodded, "Sounds like you want a revenge template. Those are my favorites!"

Samantha thought for a moment, and vehemently responded, "Hell yes!"

Amanda asked, "So what type of revenge do you wish on this individual?

"My boyfriend," Samantha said correcting Amanda.

"My fault. What type of revenge video do you want to happen to your boyfriend? And we'll need a photograph of your boyfriend, preferably full-body so we can find an actor to portray him."

Samantha thought for a moment and said, "I'd like him to be in a movie theater that has a horror movie playing. Since he'll be on his phone, it's unlikely he'll be paying attention." Samantha continued, "I want the killer in the movie to come out of the screen with his chainsaw and approach my boyfriend."

"That sounds similar to the premise of 'The Ring.'" Amanda replied.

Being the movie aficionado she was, Samantha replied, "Yes, that's kinda my inspiration."

"That sounds like a good revenge template." Amanda complimented Samantha. "Any further details you'd like to add?"

"Yes! I want the killer to have blood splatter all over his clothes and approach Thomas and ask him why he has his cell phone out in a deep and threatening voice." Samantha continued, "I want the killer to turn on his chainsaw and slash Thomas's phone to bits. At that point, Thomas will be so scared that he'll piss his pants and run out of the theater terrified. Then I want the killer to return to the movie with the patrons applauding gleefully."

"That sounds fabulous and a much better premise than 'The Ring,'" Amanda said in approval to the well-thought-out torture template. Amanda, although new to in-house pre-screening, she recognized that Samantha would be an excellent client for Mindefusement.

"That sounds like an absolute winner, Samantha. You've just successfully passed pre-screening," Amanda said. "We're going to send you a package in the mail, and I'd like you to open it immediately upon receipt. We're a bit short staffed because of that viral video you mentioned, so wait times may be longer than usual."

Impatiently, Samantha asked, "What do I do until I receive the package?"

"Just wait for the package. In the meantime, we'll set you up with a support person, probably Cassandra, and then we can flesh out your torture template into a script."

"So you think this is a doable template?" Samantha asked.

"Absolutely!" Amanda exclaimed enthusiastically. "I just wish I even had a boyfriend so I could get even with him!"

"Thanks," Samantha said blushing. She couldn't believe Amanda didn't have a boyfriend with her intense beauty and charisma.

"We'll FedEx your package with a two-day delivery, so expect it then."

"Great," Samantha said. "I can't wait."

"Any additional concerns or questions?" Amanda asked.

"Nope, I think we're good," Samantha said in a satisfied tone.

"Alright then. I hope to talk to you soon."

They both hung up.

Amanda's first solo pre-screening call made her smile with satisfaction at a job well-done. She knew it had gone well and informed the accounting department to accept the deposit, and notified support to go ahead and send Samantha the package.

Chapter 17

VERONICA

Veronica was the mother of two-year-old twins whose philandering husband left her when their third child was on the way. Veronica adored her husband and spent the first 3 months after his departure in deep depression. Eventually, Veronica moved on to resentment and anger at his betrayal, giving her the impetus not only to survive but to make a decent life for herself and her kids. Living well may be the best revenge, but Veronica wanted more.

She fantasized constantly about ending her ex-husband's life in a myriad of ways. Some days, she imagined watching him jaywalking, stepping into a pothole, getting his foot stuck, and a bus running him down leaving him as merely a bloody splotch in the street. Other times, she envisioned him catching sight of her and running after her to apologize, but suffering an excruciating heart attack before he could reach her. One of her darker fantasies involved a serial killer torturing her ex-husband until he expired.

With these fantasies in mind, Veronica discovered Mindefusement through the now infamous 'Blue Balls' torture template shared widely on the Internet. She realized that the combination of her fantasy with virtual reality by Mindefusement might just be the perfect way to satisfy her endless craving for her ex-spouse's gruesome demise. It would be the perfect fit she thought.

Mindefusement was still going through growing pains following its popularity on Reddit and YouTube. After several weeks, Veronica finally made it to the top of the waiting list Jake and Amanda were wading through. Jake assigned Amanda to be the point person for this call, as his queue was full, and he was getting weary of vexed exes and their torture templates. Amanda, on the other hand, got vicarious enjoyment from the torture templates clients thought up and was more than happy to do the pre-screening of Veronica. Amanda's first glimpse on the Google Hangout revealed an exhausted, single mom holding her infant daughter while two rambunctious toddlers romped around in the background.

Veronica introduced herself to Amanda.

"Ooh, she's so adorable!" Amanda squealed in delight on seeing the little cherub.

"Thank you!" Veronica said, "Her name is Abby."

"Hi, there you wittle bitty bundle of love! Aren't you just the prettiest itty bitty thing in the world!" Amanda in that baby-talk voice adults reserve for kids and small animals.

Abby cooed happily, and Amanda and Veronica laughed.

"They're so delightful at this age," Veronica stated, "I never want her to grow up."

"Yes, babies are just so cute and cuddly," Amanda agreed while hearing her biological clock ticking in her head. Amanda sighed inwardly then got back on track: "So let's get down to business, shall we?"

"Yes, let's get to it! I've been waiting weeks for a response!"

Amanda questioned, "So are you familiar with what we do here at Mindefusement?"

"Yes," Veronica said, "You make fantasy films for clients. It's all over the net now what you do."

"Perfect, but are you familiar with pre-screening?"

"A bit from the Reddit thread. You basically make sure that I'm a fit client before you proceed with the actual film."

"Exactly!" Amanda exclaimed. "Tell me what you have in mind for your torture template."

Veronica's fury was unleashed as she dove into the background of why she wanted to be a client.

"I want him dead. Now." Veronica stated. "He left me with three children. He's absolute scum and the poorest excuse for a human being."

Amanda, taken aback by Veronica's vehemence, questioned, "But you realize we just do fantasy, correct?"

To which Veronica replied more calmly, "Well, I DO what him dead in real life, too. But a film will have to suffice the carnage I wish would happen to my ex-husband. I don't want my kids to have to visit me in jail. Or worse yet, end up with my ex!"

Amanda, ready to reject Veronica from pre-screening, explained, "I do want you to know that this is all fantasy and you are to not do any of this in real life. This would expose Mindefusement as a co-conspirator in your ex-husband's death."

"As much as I want my ex-husband dead," Veronica explained, "I simply do not have enough energy to do it in real life. He's a slimy deadbeat and not worth the effort. Karma will come his way eventually."

"Fair enough." Amanda conceded. "So what do you want to do for your torture template?"

Veronica explained: "I see my ex-husband lying helpless on life support but totally conscious. I want him to be in excruciating pain."

Amanda asked, "So, he can still feel, hear, and see, right?"

"Yes," Veronica said. "Have you seen the movie Deadpool?"

Amanda replied, "Of course! Great movie!"

"Do you remember how they fucked with his oxygen supply and he became a mutant?"

"Yep," Amanda said.

"Well, I kinda want the same thing, however, I want my ex-husband to be killed after experiencing agonizing physical and psychological pain."

"So how do you kill your ex?" Amanda asked.

Veronica replied, "So in my fantasy, my ex-husband is on life support and in immense pain. He's on a morphine drip to alleviate his discomfort."

Amanda began her question: "So your ex is on life support and you want...."

"I want to take away his morphine drip so he can really suffer the pain," Veronica jumped in, interrupting, "He needs to have nothing to relieve his physical distress while he suffers in silence. Then drag the asshole off life support by cutting off his oxygen."

Amanda smiled and nodded approvingly.

Veronica continued, "How about a look-alike actress portraying me shutting off his oxygen supply? As he realizes he is dying, the panic and fear in his eyes will be very satisfying. And just before he passes out, she turns the oxygen back on, and he revives. To save some money, we can do a loop of this several times. For the finale, we cut to the view through his eyes where the look-alike doesn't turn the oxygen back on, and everything fades to black. At this point, his body will shake and do the death rattle. And have him convulsing the entire time. I need to see the shock and helplessness in his eyes as his oxygen is repeatedly turned off. Perhaps a close-up of his face?"

"Yes! Basically, slow torture by repeated suffocation?" Amanda asked. "Yeah, I suppose that sounds like Deadpool to me, but instead your ex-husband is at a regular hospital on life support."

Veronica smiled gleefully, still holding her newborn, and exclaimed: "Just make sure the actress is smiling and maybe giggling a little, and it will be perfect!"

"Great," Amanda said. "We'll set you up with a Mindefusement account and mail you the package."

"What's in the package?" Veronica asked.

"It's just a simple tablet. It's a way to get hold of us securely. And when your video is finished, the tablet provides a way to watch it."

"Fantastic!" Veronica enthusiastically responded.

"I'm happy to accept you as a Mindefusement client." Amanda smirked, "This should be a fun one. What about your ex in real life?"

Veronica thought for a bit and finally said, "I really want to see him dead, but the kids don't need a dead parent and the other parent in jail. You're providing a great service here, saving multiple lives."

"That's what we like to do here," Amanda said dryly. "Although if your ex-husband kicks the bucket in real life, then that's just too bad. Would you do this in real life if your ex-husband was on life support?"

"Honestly," Veronica replied, "I wouldn't have the guts. But I'd probably visit him and spit in his food or something."

Amanda laughed.

"That being said, yes, I do really wish he would die with a lot of pain and suffering rather than dying in his sleep in old age," Veronica said coldly.

"Me, too," Amanda said agreeing, "Your ex-husband sounds like a dirtbag. What decent human being abandons his wife and three small children?"

Veronica smiled, "Yep, three crazy kids. But I hold my own."

"Looks like it," Amanda replied. She asked, "Anything else?"

"No, I think we're good."

"Okay then. Welcome to Mindefusement and have a great rest of your day. We'll mail the package shortly and get you set up."

Veronica smiled, "You have no idea how happy I am right now!"

"Glad to be of help," Amanda replied. "We'll be talking to each other soon with your finished product." Amanda gave a final wave to the baby in Veronica's arms and said, "Again, welcome to Mindefusement. I wish you the best."

"Thank you," Veronica said smiling. They both exited the Google Hangout.

Chapter 18

THE COPYCAT

A shley was in the mailroom sorting mail when the FedEx package arrived addressed to George Shiner, CEO of Mindefusement. The mail clerk added it to the other mail in the small cart she used to distribute the mail and headed up to the CEO's office to deliver it and various newspapers he subscribed to.

The CEO's door was open, and Ashley walked in cheerfully saying, "Good morning, Mr. Shiner. You have a package from New York," as she placed the box in front of him.

"From New York?" Mr. Shiner asked with suspicion. Mr. Shiner examined the package and responded, "Thank you, Ashley. Do you have a box-cutter?"

"Sure thing, Mr. Shiner. Let me open it for you." Ashley deftly slit open the packing tape, opened the box, and removed the bubble wrap that was on top of the contents. As soon as she did that, she let out a piercing scream that could be heard in the far corners of the building. The CEO merely gasped as his eyes opened wide at the contents.

Inside were three zip-lock bags. One was full of blood, hair, and what appeared to be a severed finger. The second bag contained a USB drive. Inside the third bag was an envelope with the CEO's name typed on it followed by "Personal and Confidential" on the line below.

Ashley's terrified scream had brought the other employees of Mindefusement rushing into Mr. Shiner's office. The CEO, with other employees hovering, directed the bodyguard to immediately call the police.

The bodyguard briefly described the contents of the package, and he was advised that no one should touch the package or its contents to avoid contaminating evidence. He was also told that the police were being dispatched to investigate and that he should secure the building. No one was to enter or leave until the police got there.

When the police arrived, they were as dumbfounded as the CEO. The officer in charge asked the CEO, "Do you know anything about this package or where it came from?" The CEO replied, "Apparently from New York according to the tracking information."

The officer replied, "Do you know anyone in New York that has a vendetta against you? Or the company?"

"No," the CEO lied.

The officer said, "We need to get the crime scene division in to look at this," and got on his radio. "Let me talk to Lt. Taylor Miller." After 20 seconds or so, he continued:

"Taylor, we have a mysterious package that suggests possible torture and/or murder. We need you to call in the crime scene investigation team on this one."

Lt. Miller replied, " Okay, take custody of the package, and interview anyone that did or might have any knowledge about it. Do you know where the package originated from?"

"New York," the officer replied. At that point, Lt. Miller said, "Well, the package crossed state lines, and that makes this an interstate crime. We need to call in the F.B.I. in on this. Hang out where you are and wait for them to arrive. In the meantime, interview the employees of the company."

The policeman got off the radio and informed Mr. Shiner, "We have the F.B.I. coming to check out the package. While we're waiting for them, I need to interview anyone that came in contact with this package or was in the building when it arrived. Do you have a conference room or office we can use?"

The CEO responded, "Yes, we have a boardroom you may use for the interviews."

The police officer started by interviewing Ashley from the mailroom. "Please state your name and spell it for me."

Ashley replied, still distraught, "Ashley Davis. A-S-H-L-E-Y D-A-V-I-S."

"Okay, Ms. Davis, do you mind if I record our conversation for accuracy? You are free to stop this interview at any time if you feel uncomfortable."

Ashley responded, "That's fine. I really know nothing other than that this package showed up this morning addressed to Mr. Shiner, our CEO, and I took it up to him with the rest of his mail."

The officer replied, "That's fine. Can you give me your home address and a good contact number? Also, how long have you worked at this company?"

Ashley responded by giving her address, cell phone number, and said, "I've worked here for about six months."

The officer questioned, "Have there been any other packages from New York or elsewhere with 'unusual' contents?"

"No," Ashley replied, "Not that I know of. This would be the first."

The officer walked Ashley through the sequence of events from the time the FedEx delivery person left the package through when she delivered and opened it for the CEO. Satisfied with her answers, he released her from the interview and called in the next employee. The CEO told Ashley she could go home since she was upset and the mailroom was shut down for the day.

The CEO was the next up for interrogation but asked to be interviewed later so he could contact the company's board of directors and Julie Biggs, general counsel, who was in Dallas visiting her brother.

The next employee interviewed was Jason. He denied having any contact with anyone in New York and could not provide any insight on why someone would send such an ominous package. Next up was Jake who likewise denied contact with anyone from New York. Cassandra was out of the office taking a vacation day, so she wasn't around to dispute either Jake's or Jason's statements. After several hours and interviews, no employee admitted having any dealings with New York until they interviewed Ben Hammond, head of accounting, He revealed that Jason had submitted several questionable vouchers and receipts for reimbursement from Manhattan about one month earlier. Ben went to get the records for the police just as the agents from the F.B.I. arrived.

The F.B.I. agents sat down with the local officers to learn what information the police officers had obtained. The local police conveyed the information that Jason had lied about having any connection with New York. They provided the F.B.I. with the records from accounting, and provided information which showed Mr. Shiner had approved the dubious vouchers and receipts submitted by Jason. It was at this point the feds took over the investigation from the local police.

One of the federal agents brought Jason back into the conference room for further questioning. After giving Jason his Miranda rights and advising him that they had proof that he had been in New York recently, the lead agent asked: "So tell us what you were doing in New York?" Jason invoked his right to counsel and asked for representation. He was taken into custody.

The feds called in the CEO. Special Agent Andrew Harris conducted the interview. George Shiner remained calm. He admitted that his daughter Renee was in New York City attending school but denied having approved Jason's expenses that were submitted to accounting. He stated that Jason had been looking at an additional service he had previously proposed to the board of directors that had been scotched a few months earlier. However, Jason was still hot to promote the new product and went to New York for further research to support his suggestion. After a tense hour of trying to trip the CEO up, the feds released him figuring that additional corroborative testimony would be easily obtained.

Back at the Dallas headquarters, the forensic team agents examined the package. The blood was examined, and it was found to be non-human. The hair was human but they found no DNA match in the system. It could've been obtained from a hairbrush, a comb, shower drain, or a pillow. The finger was real but did not match the DNA of the hair. The envelope addressed to Mr. Shiner was examined for any fingerprints (there were none) and opened carefully. It was a self-stick envelope so there was no saliva for testing. The letter inside had been printed on an HP Officejet, which was impossible to track down. It was found that the USB drive contained only one file, which was an MP4 video.

The MP4 on the USB drive was played by the forensic team. What was on the video was disturbing, to say the least. A Jane Doe with her face obscured was filmed answering her door. She was immediately gagged and bound by the unknown assailant, and a violent rape commenced. The assailant filmed the lady's throat being slashed as she gurgled on her own blood. The assailant then filmed a finger being sliced off and held up the finger in full view of the camera. He then filmed the collection of blood, hair, the finger, and then doused the body with bleach to cover up any DNA evidence.

Mr. Shiner was called into the F.B.I. headquarters in

Dallas for further questioning. He was allowed to read the note. The note read, "I'm on to you, George Shiner. Consider this the beginning of the end for you and Mindefusement." Mr. Shiner was then allowed to view the video. The CEO immediately recognized this as a copycat killing. He spoke, "My son Richard was convicted of a crime matching this video a few years ago. Clearly, the perpetrator is trying to make this a personal threat. This is a copycat killing to implicate me and destroy my company."

Agent Harris then informed the CEO that the video was a fake using CGI which forensics had confirmed. Perplexed, the CEO was stunned into silence.

Agent Harris asked, "Is this the first threat against you or the business that you received?"

The CEO responded, "None. Well, in the past we had an employee assaulted, but no threats have been received since then." Inwardly, the CEO trembled at the thought that perhaps Marc had family or friends who had a vendetta against him personally with the mission of destroying Mindefusement.

Andrew spoke, "Well obviously you have someone with a serious grudge against you. The video is a fake, but there is nothing fake about the note. Are you SURE you there is nobody in New York who wants revenge against you or your company?"

The CEO sat silently, watching the video again, "No."

Andrew asked, "Your employee, Jason Wilson, lied about having any connection to New York, but he was there a little over a month ago. Accounting told us about the questionable expense vouchers he submitted."

Mr. Shiner swallowed hard and replied: "I had and have no knowledge of any employee that was in New York."

"Okay then," Andrew responded, knowing the CEO was lying. "Let us know in the event you receive any other suspicious packages. This may not be the last."

"Yes, sir," the CEO agreed, quaking in his shoes, realizing he was totally fucked.

The CEO left the F.B.I. headquarters and returned to Mindefusement. The CEO called a meeting in the main boardroom with Jake and Julie, who had returned from visiting her brother.

The CEO stated matter-of-factly: "So we have someone who knows that Mindefusement was involved in Marc Brown's suicide. I received a package with blood, hair, a severed finger, and a thumb drive containing a gruesome and violent but fake video of a rape and murder similar that was a copycat of the one committed by my son, Richard. That brings me to the obvious question: Did Marc have a living relative, friend, or lover who could do such a thing?"

Jake responded, "Marc broke up with his girlfriend to pursue Renee, but he had a quite a few living relatives: his father, mother, and numerous siblings. Maybe one of them wants revenge for Marc's suicide?"

"Whatever the case," the CEO said, "We have a serious situation if someone wants to tarnish Mindefusement."

Julie, who had been silent since the beginning of the meeting, nodded in agreement, and said, "It seems someone wants revenge for Marc's death. The actual relationship to Marc isn't relevant. What did the note say?"

"It said that the person who sent the package wanted to destroy Mindefusement and me, personally," the CEO responded.

"Well, that's not hard to foresee," Julie concluded. "We destroyed a man's reputation causing him to commit suicide. The subject of the stalking was your daughter. This is all easily traceable back to us. It isn't a surprise that you, the company, and anyone with any knowledge of the stalking is in deep shit."

"What do you suggest, Julie?" the CEO asked.

"You should have fired Jake and Jason immediately after discovering their actions. Now, you, me and anyone with any knowledge, will be considered co-conspirators either before or after the fact. We all need to lawyer up."

The CEO responded, "Let's play this game as wait-and-see. Maybe the package we received was just a warning."

"Or it is just the beginning," Julie warned sharply.

"Let's adjourn this meeting. This has already been a long day. Let's get back to work."

Everyone in the room nodded and left the room and inwardly thought about how they could save their own skin.

Chapter 19
REVENGE

William "Memphis" Brown was Marc's next older and the sibling with the closest relationship to him. Memphis was distraught and enraged over Marc's suicide. He had received a cryptic email from Marc just before the suicide. The email provided Marc's access to a program that contained all of Marc's passwords. Memphis wasn't satisfied with the authorities cursory investigation of the circumstances surrounding his brother's suicide. He knew the email from Marc was a plea from the grave for Memphis to find the real reason for his death, and Memphis vowed to get to the bottom of what happened.

He visited Marc's apartment in New York to find the apartment in shambles. He dug through the disorder until he found Marc's phone, charged it, and began to peruse its contents. What he found was disturbing. Marc had messaged a girl named Renee Shiner hundreds and hundreds of times. Memphis also found one of Marc's last text messages admitting that he was a stalker. Despite the fact that it appeared Marc was relentlessly stalking Renee, Memphis knew Marc too well to believe he would ever send out a text like that. And that text message had gone out to hundreds of numbers that were not in Marc's contact list. Memphis concluded that his brother's cell phone had obviously been hacked. The questions were: Why and by whom?

Memphis was a programmer. His special skills he used in his profession were to secure clients' websites from fraudulent hacking by third-parties including those with complaints and grudges against the clients. Memphis quickly concluded that Marc was the object of a reputation destruction campaign.

To answer the two questions of who and why, Memphis started by Googling Renee Shiner. He learned through LinkedIn and other social media that Renee had worked at Marc's Keggles while she attended college. This seemed odd since he discovered Renee was the daughter of the wealthy George Shiner, one of whose many business ventures included a company known as Mindefusement. The company had operated under until recently. He discovered the "Blue Balls" video on the net. Memphis concluded that Mindefusement was in the business of making high-tech fantasy films for clients.

Memphis pulled up the Mindefusement contact page. He quickly realized that if a potential client successfully completed the interview process and had sufficient

resources to pay the steep deposit, he or she could vicar-
iously enjoy watching whatever evil or twisted fantasy
come to life. The hack of Marc's cell phone and the dissem-
ination of the text that he was a stalker using reputation
destruction could mean that Mindefusement had an additional product in the wings for clients.

Memphis figured that Mindefusement was responsible for his brother's beating and hospitalization. Marc had
been very evasive when talking to the police in the hospital,
and with the number of muggings in NYC, no suspects
were identified. One of Marc's passwords included an
online link to the security footage at Keggles stored
remotely off-site. Memphis checked the security footage
of the night of Marc's hospitalization and could make out
two large males exiting a vehicle as Marc locked up for the
night. Using visual enhancement, Memphis. used a reverse
Google image search. He discovered the two goons were
employed as bouncers at a couple of local bars.

Memphis visited the nightclubs where the bouncers
worked. He had checked out their criminal records and
found that both had prior arrests for assault and battery.
He took pictures of them for his records.

He approached one of the bouncers on a slow night
and point-blank asked him, "Look, I know you beat the
shit out of my brother who worked at Keggles..."

The bouncer interrupted, "Fuck off!" The bouncer's
facial expressions suggested he was guilty.

"You hospitalized my brother, you asshole, but I'm
not here about that. My brother is dead. He committed suicide because someone hacked his phone, got him

fired, and destroyed his life. While you and a buddy beat the shit out of him, I know someone paid you to do the job. I want to know who hired you to do the job since I'm damned sure they are the ones responsible for him taking his life." Memphis responded heatedly.

"I'll tell what I know for a small fee."

Memphis pulled out a crisp hundred dollar bill. "Is this enough?"

"I was thinking more like five c-notes," the bouncer replied.

Memphis pulled out another hundred and replied, "Let's hear some information with what I have and I'll determine if it's worth the five hundred dollars or not."

The bouncer took the money and replied, "All I know is I got a call from a guy named Jason. He said he needed some muscle to threaten some creep that was stalking a college chick."

Memphis took out another hundred dollar bill, handed it to the bouncer, and continued: "What was the college chick's name?"

After a slight hesitation, the bouncer replied, "Renee."

"How did you know where to find my brother?"

"This Jason guy told us where the dude worked and told me to make it clear that if the guy ever came near the girl or contacted her again, we would return and do more than talk. Your brother was a real jerk, and he needed more than just a tongue lashing."

Memphis' temper boiled, but he realized he had more questions that need answers. "How did this Jason find you and contact you?"

"Bouncers don't get paid all that well. I listed services for those needing muscle on Craigslist that goes to a burner cell. I can give you his number. I still have it on my burner. It was a 972 area code if I remember correctly."

"That works," Memphis replied. Satisfied with the bouncer's response, Memphis took out two more hundred dollar bills and handed them to the bouncer.

"Thanks, that's all I needed to know." Memphis replied. Memphis Googled the 972 area code. It was a Dallas area code. This information put Memphis a step closer to confirming Mindefusement's involvement with Marc's suicide, but he still needed more evidence.

In addition to the video cameras inside the store, there were two outside cameras. Memphis checked the security footage of the day when Marc's infamous text was sent. He discovered a suspicious-looking van with an antenna array parked across the street. His hunch was that Mindefusement set up a fake cell network to intercept Marc's cell phone. He also discovered the Facebook video of customers accosting Marc.

It just seemed too convenient for Marc's attention to Renee Shiner, daughter of Mindefusement's CEO, Marc's hospitalization, the hacking, and the reputation destruction leading to his death to be coincidental. Memphis had the information gathered from the bouncer and the surveillance video of the van outside Keggles when the text was sent. It wasn't much of a leap to conclude that Marc's reputation destruction was engineered by Renee's father's company. He was now hell-bent on destroying Mindefusement and began to formulate his plan.

Memphis researched Renee's brother Richard. He discovered the brother was serving a life term without the possibility of parole in the maximum security prison in Huntsville, Texas for the crimes of rape and murder. Memphis read the public accounts of the crime. Memphis decided to do a copycat video of Richard's rape and murder to gauge the reaction of George Shiner and Mindefusement as a whole. He enlisted the help of his girlfriend to make a fake rape video. With video editing skills, Memphis used a GoPro camera to visit his girlfriend. He gagged and bound her, and commenced a fake rape. He then fake-sliced her throat and used pigs blood to cover the crime scene. He then doused a look-a-like dummy with bleach to make it look like he was covering up the crime scene. He tried to make the video look as real as possible, but without the high-tech resources available to Mindefusement, it was obvious the video was a fake.

He enlisted the help of a friend at the morgue to get a severed human finger. He then used a contact at his local barber shop to get real human hair that matched his girlfriend's. With the video and assets completed, he sent a package of pig's blood, hair, a severed finger, and his video to Mindefusement addressed to George Shiner. He added a typed note to the package informing the CEO that the sender was on to Mindefusement's antics.

Memphis was more than a little pissed that he had to conduct the investigation since the police had done nothing. He formulated a plan for his own reputation destruction of Mindefusement and its CEO which would follow after Mindefusement received his FedEx package.

Since "Blue Balls" had blown Mindefusement's anonymity, Memphis knew there must be a lot more videos out there somewhere. He scoured the net for anything or anyone connected to Mindefusement. He found some advertisements for the company, but that was about it. He browsed the Mindefusement website's source code. He found his connection to Jason, who left an HTML comment saying he coded the website. He also found a GitHub profile that was linked to Mindefusement. Most of the repositories were private, but he did find one that was public that had foolishly published their Amazon S3 keys.

He quickly logged in to the Amazon S3 account and was amazed at how little security they had for the completed videos. All of their videos were in one place, listed in buckets based on the client's name. He was appalled by the graphic content of the first few videos he watched. By leaking the videos, he would destroy both Mindefusement's and the clients' reputations. He made the entire S3 account world-viewable, published the list, and sent them out to a few hacker groups he was a part of. He also downloaded the videos and created a public Dropbox where the videos could be viewed should some-one at Mindefusement get wind of the now-public videos.

Memphis anonymously contacted a few national news and Dallas outlets and shared the list of the videos along with his findings and Mindefusement's address. He also distributed the videos and his findings to the federal authorities in New York and Texas.

Confident that he had delivered the death blow to

Mindefusement and its CEO, Memphis sat back to watch the drama unfold. He smirked that his intermediate hacking skills would be responsible to perhaps bring justice to his brother's untimely death by suicide. He regretted that Marc hadn't reached out to him before he took his life. However Marc, in his final moments, had put his trust in Memphis to deliver the justice and vindication he deserved.

The revenge wasn't complete, however. Memphis had further plans for destruction.

Chapter 20

INFAMY

Julie was about to have one hell of a night. She received a frantic phone call from the CEO shortly after 3:30 am. Groggy, Julie answered her mobile.

"They've been leaked."

Still in that gray zone of conscious thought between sleep and waking up, Julie asked, "What's been leaked?"

The CEO responded in an urgent voice, "All of the videos have been leaked."

Julie's adrenaline immediately began pumping, and she was instantly awake. Hoping that Mr. Shiner was exaggerating, she needed confirmation, "All of our clients' videos have been leaked?"

"Yes," the CEO responded. "I need you to get to the office right away!"

Julie quickly showered which helped to clear her

head and focus on the catastrophe. She dressed quickly in comfortable clothes but grabbed her blue suit and make-up just in case. Driving just five miles over the speed limit with little traffic, she made the 20-minute drive to the Mindefusement headquarters in Frisco by 4:30 am.

Julie walked swiftly to the CEO's office and entered without knocking. "So what happened?"

"All of the videos we've ever created have been leaked to the public. I can't imagine a worst-case scenario that would top this. With Jason gone, we have no one here who can fix this," said the CEO as he uncharacteristically paced behind his magnificent desk.

"What the fuck!" Julie exclaimed. "I need coffee and a lot of it before dealing with this."

Julie left the room and soon returned with two styrofoam cups full of black coffee. She handed one to the CEO.

"Thank you," the CEO said, accepting the coffee. He asked, "So what do we do now?"

"Short answer? We're fucked! The leaked videos are tied to our clients. Their reputations are destroyed, and they will come after the company. Not to mention that Mindefusement's reputation as a company is blown as well due to the content of those videos."

"So what can we do to mitigate our damages or liability?" the CEO asked.

"Obviously, our clients won't be happy about this. We need Jake in here with suggestions on how to deal with our clients. Is he on his way in?" Julie asked.

"Yes, we 911'd him. He should be here shortly," the CEO explained. He continued, "Just do what you can to minimize the already extensive damage that has occurred." the CEO said.

Julie asked, "There's nothing I can do. Lawyer up. We can expect reporters. We can expect protesters. We can be sued by our clients because the leaked videos can be easily traced back to them. We're in a world of shit."

At that point, Jake rushed into the CEO's office and announced, "Wow, there are already two reporters out there!"

"Did they ask any questions?" Julie asked.

"Oh yeah. They asked me who I was and what I did for Mindefusement. I kept my mouth shut and just kept walking. So the videos were leaked online?" Jake asked almost rhetorically.

The CEO took a sip of his coffee and responded, "Yep, all of them. It's like someone has a vendetta against us. I have no idea who did this or why, but it happened none-theless. I think I need to go talk to some of the reporters."

"I advise that you shut the fuck up and stay where you are!" Julie warned.

"No, I can handle a few reporters." the CEO responded.

Julie disagreed, "Until we can go through ALL the possible questions the reporters will ask and have prepared answers, you are totally unprepared to meet the press. The leaked videos may be just one of a number of issues they will question you about. If you are unprepared to address all issues or even look like you are dodging a question, it will bite you and the company in the ass."

Unfortunately, since the CEO was shaken by the copycat video, his business acumen was impaired, and he took this as a personal attack. The CEO ignored Julie's advice. The CEO left the office accompanied by two of his security detail.

When he stepped into the parking lot, he saw half a dozen news vans. He also saw there were a couple of dozen protesters carrying signs such as "Baby Killers" and "You're Going to Hell."

An investigative journalist named Kathryn Borne hustled to be the first to question Mr. Shiner with a cameraman by her side. She asked point-blank, "So you're in the business of making fantasy videos for clients, correct?"

The CEO didn't hesitate to respond. Truthfully, he said, "Yes, our clients pay us to make fantasy videos. It's unfortunate that the videos were leaked. We value our clients and their privacy. We will prosecute those who hacked us to the full extent of the law both civilly and criminally."

Kathryn asked, "So you're just in the business of fantasy, correct? Nothing in real life?"

"We are in the business of making videos for our clients, and that's all. Our business does not do anything in 'real' life. We provide these 'realistic' videos as a way to provide an outlet for our clients, closure if you will. They provide the basic storyline, and we use CGI and actors for the fantasy videos. The goal is to PREVENT the reality or provide closure."

"Interesting…" Kathryn paused. Then she dropped a bombshell, "And you're familiar with a man named Marc Brown?"

"Marc who?" the CEO asked, trying his best to still

the pounding in his chest when he heard the name. He realized that he should have heeded Julie's advice and stayed in his office.

"Marc Brown, from New York. He committed suicide shortly after he was hospitalized by what he described to the police as an assault by two large males."

"What does this have to do with me or Mindefusement?" the CEO asked trying to stall for time to formulate a plausible response.

"He was in contact with your daughter, was he not?"

The CEO replied, "My daughter and I had a falling out due to her choice of majors. We aren't in close communication."

"So you're saying Mindefusement wasn't responsible for hospitalizing the man and hacking his phone to send out a damning text message to hundreds of people, getting him fired, destroying his reputation, and leading to his suicide?"

The CEO made no response.

The reporter continued, "Marc Brown was in constant contact with your daughter. In fact, he appeared to be stalking her. You don't have any knowledge of either you personally or Mindefusement going the extra mile to use muscle to dissuade him from contact with your daughter or to destroy this man's reputation? I think the ownership of your company and a man stalking your daughter is a little bit coincidental, don't you think? I also received a package that appears to definitively link Mindefusement to Marc's hospitalization and suicide."

The CEO, paused before he responded, "If anyone

from Mindefusement pursued this man, he will be terminated and turned over to the authorities. I can assure you
that my daughter Renee never contacted me about any
stalker. If she had, I would have hired her a lawyer to
obtain a VPO and provided her with a bodyguard."

"Is that your answer? That Mindefusement had no
knowledge?" the reporter asked sarcastically.

The CEO replied, "I'm in charge of Mindefusement
and monitor all of its day to day business. If something
occurred that is outside the Mindefusement mission of
making fantasy videos, then that something occurred
without my knowledge or consent."

Getting frustrated, Kathryn asked, "Exactly how much
do you personally control your Mindefusement staff?
Client videos have been made public by an anonymous
person as well as provided to news outlets such as us. Add
that to the obvious connection between your company, you,
and your daughter and the physical and emotional beating of Marc Brown that led to his suicide, and it appears
Mindefusement and you personally are in a precarious
situation."

"Look," said the CEO with growing impatience, "At
this point, we haven't had the opportunity to determine
whether the leak was an inside job or not. The leaking
of the videos is detrimental to our clientele. When we
can determine who leaked the videos, I reiterate that we
will take all appropriate civil and criminal actions available. I have already addressed your allegations regarding
Marc Brown."

Kathryn smirked, "I can tell you're lying. But that's

okay. We'll let the authorities handle the legal side of this. According to the package I received, you're in very hot water."

The CEO concluded the interview saying: "I have nothing further to add at this time. We have to determine how the videos were leaked, by whom, and the reason it was done. We will provide you with additional information when our investigation is concluded. Thank you." Mr. Shiner quickly turned around and hurried back to the safety of the Mindefusement office as more protesters showed up. They began chanting, "Avenge Marc's Death!"

"Julie, Jake! Meeting now!" the CEO shouted as he hurried past his employees on the way to the boardroom.

In the meeting, the CEO announced, "The leak is now the least of our worries. Marc's assault, reputation destruction, and subsequent suicide have been traced back to Mindefusement according to information received by the reporter who confronted me."

Julie refrained from screaming: "I fucking told you this would happen!" Instead, she took a slow deep breath, and asked in a level voice, "Tell me exactly what the reporter said and how you responded."

The CEO recounted the accusatory statements and his responses. He added sarcastically, "I am sure we will be regaled with choice incriminating soundbites from the interview playing on the morning news shows shortly." The CEO continued, "I plan to give a brief update of the situation at a press conference tomorrow."

The attendees were speechless. Finally, Julie broke the stunned silence to ask, "What exactly do you propose to talk about?"

The CEO responded, "I'm not sure yet. We need to find out exactly what was in the package sent to the press and where it came from. It may shed some light on who leaked the videos." After a short pause, he continued, "I'll want to address the leaking of the videos and the steps we are taking on behalf of our clients. Jake, it's your job to contact every one of our clients and inform them of the leak."

"The leak ties the videos to the clients. Some will just be embarrassed, but others will have their reputations destroyed, lose their jobs, or be ostracized by friends and family. One or two may choose the solution Marc Brown did. On the other hand, some will be glad their video masterpieces are public. What the hell am I supposed to say to the damned clients to reassure them? I'm a salesman, not a therapist. What do you want me to do? I'm not into public relations." Jake responded with an edge of hysteria in his voice.

The CEO replied impatiently, "Apologize, sympathize, cry, laugh… I don't care what it takes. You're a salesman. Use your persuasive skills to make our clients happy. Bribe them if necessary."

"It won't help. Our clients are fucked," Jake emphatically retorted.

The CEO, seething in anger, shouted, "You and Jason fucked the company and me personally when you went rogue in assisting Renee in deterring Marc's stalking. Your association with Marc and this mystery package we received and the one sent to the press could well be the end of Mindefusement. The leaking of the videos is unfortunate, but it's secondary to the public learning of the connection between Marc's suicide and our company."

Just as the CEO finished his sentence, the F.B.I. entered the building with a no-knock warrant. Special Agent Andrew Harris entered the boardroom and served the warrant to the CEO. Agent Harris said, "We have evidence persons associated with Mindefusement have conspired and committed crimes including but not limited to hacking cell phone communications, payment to intimidate others through violence, and crimes involving interstate commerce. This is a search and seizure warrant authorizing us to confiscate all records, laptops, servers, and obtain records of all past and current employees and contractors including maintenance personnel. We will also need to interrogate all employees who are now on the premises. Please have everyone assemble in the conference room. We'll conduct interviews in our office."

The CEO's confidence was shaken by the abrupt appearance of Agent Harris and the CEO's employees saw the end of Mindefusement and his own career. Meekly, the CEO handed the warrant over to Julie.

Julie quickly but carefully read the warrant and exclaimed: "This is utter bullshit! What grounds do you have?"

Agent Harris replied, "We have received competent evidence that individuals associated with this company are responsible for the aggravated assault of an individual known as Marc Brown in New York City. Additionally, it appears individuals either employed by or contracted to and paid by this company hacked a cell phone tower."

Julie let out her best Jack Bauer scoff but otherwise made no response.

Agent Harris continued, "You, Jake Roberts, and Mr. Shiner will be interrogated in our Dallas office. All current and former employees will be interrogated by an agent at the local police station."

Agent Harris told one of the agents to inform the employees who were currently segregated in the conference room that they were being transported to the local police station for questioning. there.

Jake, Julie, and the CEO were taken in separate vehicles to the FBI office in Dallas. They were placed in three virtually identical interrogation rooms and offered coffee, tea, water, or soft drinks. Agent Harris began first with Julie. After asking her name, address, position with Mindefusement, length of employment with Mindefusement, prior employment, education, and other innocuous questions, he asked: "When did you first hear the name Marc Brown?" Julie immediately requested the presence of counsel, stopping the interrogation. Harris knew that she wouldn't fall for the sympathetic: "We know this wasn't your idea. You probably didn't know anything until after the fact, etc." so he didn't try to eke out any additional information. He had Julie taken into custody. He knew that she was smart enough to know that if a lawyer tries to represent herself, she has a fool for a lawyer as well as a fool for a client. Julie knew she was an accomplice after the fact, and the best outcome she could hope for was to negotiate an immunity deal or at least a suspended sentence in consideration for her testimony,

Agent Harris had permitted Jake to cool his heels in the interrogation room for well over an hour before questioning him. The usual cocky Jake was pretty much a basket case at that point. Agent Harris asked him the same innocuous background questions he had asked Julie after Mirandizing him. Jake relaxed somewhat, at which point, Harris looked him dead in the eye and asked: "When did you have your initial contact with Renee Shiner about Marc Brown stalking her?" Jake began shaking from head to toe and started sobbing. "I didn't intend that Marc should be harmed. Those goons were just supposed to give him a stiff warning to stay away from Renee!"

Jake was pretty much scared shitless. Agent Harris exuded empathy: "I know you intended no actual harm. You're just someone who cared about a young girl in New York without friends and family around to protect her and give advice. We know that Jason was the guy who made the arrangements for the confrontation as well as hiring the expert to hack the cell tower. We also know that others knew about both the beating and hacking. We want to know who knew, when they knew, and how much they knew. It's in your best interest to cooperate with us."

Jake, a broken man, began to spill his guts.

The CEO sat alone in another interrogation room. The chair was uncomfortable. It was designed to be. At first, Mr. Shiner's primary emotion was anger. Anger at Jason's impetuous actions, going beyond his authority and the Mindefusement mission. Anger at Jake for going along with Jason's plan and then trying to cover up for him. Anger at Renee for running off to New York to go to drama school. Anger at himself for not paying more attention to his daughter.

An hour passed while Agent Harris interrogated Julie briefly, and Jake at length. Other than the chair the CEO sat in, two more chairs across from him, the table between them, and a fourth chair in a corner of the room, there was nothing of interest other than a clock above what he assumed was a one-way mirror. He presumed he was being observed. His anger had been spent, and the CEO was bored… and tired. He got up and walked around the table a couple of times and then stopped in front of the mirror. Childishly, he stuck out his tongue, then shouted "Fuck you!" while shooting the finger at his reflection. He had no way of knowing whether anyone was actually out there watching, but seeing himself in the mirror made the CEO laugh.

Seconds later, an agent entered the room and asked if the CEO would like some coffee, a soda, or water while he waited. He asked: "What's taking Agent Harris so long? I need to get back to Mindefusement and help deal with my clients and the public relations crisis."

"Agent Harris will be here momentarily." the agent replied. "Are you sure you don't want anything?"

"A coffee would be great," the CEO replied.

The agent left the room and returned with Agent Harris and a styrofoam cup filled with coffee. Agent Harris spoke, "Sorry for your wait. Your employee, Jake has been very cooperative in providing us with information regarding Marc's assault and the hacking of the cell phone tower. We have his testimony as well as additional evidence of your involvement. You are under arrest…"

The pounding of his heart was all Mr. Shiner could hear as Agent Harris continued: "You have the right to remain silent. Anything you say can and will be used against you in a court of law. You have the right to an attorney. If you cannot afford an attorney, one will be provided for you. Do you understand these rights?"

The CEO nodded as the other agent handcuffed him. He was taken to a holding cell.

Chapter 21

THE INDICTMENTS

Jason Wilson's attorney informed him that he was most assuredly facing both state and federal charges in New York. The attorney told Jason there was absolutely no hope of avoiding a conviction. At best, the attorney might be able to work out a deal for a reduced sentence in the federal criminal case in exchange for Jason waiving extradition and providing his full cooperation. The attorney approached F.B.I. Agent Harris with a proposal to present to the United States Attorney for the Southern District of New York. The prosecutor responded that any deal was dependent on what information Jason could provide and whether it could be verified. Jason waived extradition and was flown to New York in the custody of Agent Harris for interrogation.

Jason's interrogation was videotaped in New York.

He spilled the beans on how he had received the contact through a call to Mindefusement's support representative, Cassandra Jenkins, a high school friend of Renee Shiner. He provided quite a lot of detail on Renee Shiner who had initiated that call. Jason had no qualms in implicating Jake Roberts. He told of Jake's involvement in hiring the bouncers and how they agreed to hire some muscle to intimidate Marc Brown to stay away from Renee. Jason's story agreed with Jake's rendition to the F.B.I. that the bouncers were hired to talk to Marc rather than to physically harm him.

Jason told the F.B.I. of Renee's subsequent contact with Jake after Marc recovered from the assault, and substantiated that Marc was only temporarily deterred from stalking Renee. He went into detail about a meeting in the CEO's office where he had proposed rolling out a new product line for Mindefusement dubbed reputation destruction for those clients who wanted more than just a fantasy video of awful things happening to an enemy. Jason provided the names of all those who were present and what was said during that meeting. Julie Biggs, Mindefusement's general counsel, was vehemently opposed to the proposal, and the project was not approved. After everyone other than Jason and Jake had departed, the CEO had indicated he might consider its use if the appropriate situation arose.

Jason and Jake decided Marc's persistent stalking of Renee was an ideal test case for the use of reputation destruction. Jason provided the name and contact information of the technician he hired to hack Marc's cell phone and the cell tower. He admitted that no one other than Jake knew about the trip to New York until after the fact. Jason thoroughly covered the issues accounting had in paying his vouchers, Jake and the CEO's involvement in getting them paid, and when and what information Julie Biggs had received.

It became clear that there was sufficient evidence to call a grand jury for the purpose of obtaining indictments against Jason Wilson, Jake Roberts, Julie Biggs, George Shiner, and possibly others through the testimony. The grand jury assembled at the Daniel Patrick Moynihan United States Courthouse in New York, New York.

The witnesses the Assistant United States Attorney (AUSA) had subpoenaed included Renee Shiner, Cassandra Jenkins, Ben Hammond (head of Mindefusement's accounting department), Francisco "Frankie" Esposito, who was one of the bouncers, the hacking technician (named Michael Lee), and Marc Brown's direct superior Antonio Rivera. Jason was currently being held at Rikers on state charges, and the AUSA intended to run Jason's videotaped interrogation for the grand jury. The 23 grand jurors watched Jason's deposition, which was played in full for the grand jury.

The AUSA, Edward K. Zavoina, called Cassandra Jenkins as the first witness to testify. She had been offered an immunity deal from federal charges for her involvement in exchange for her testimony. Zavoina began his questioning: "State your name for the record."

"Cassandra Jenkins," Cassandra replied.

"And where are you currently employed?"

"I work as a support technician for Mindefusement based in Frisco, Texas. I work with our clients to develop their fantasies that are eventually turned into short videos."

Zavoina asked, "How do you know Renee Shiner?"

"Renee was my friend from high school," Cassandra responded.

"When and why did she contact you at Mindefusement?"

Cassandra replied, "Renee called me on my cell phone a couple of months ago. She told me she was being hounded by a stalker and gave me examples of the stalker's intrusion into her private life. I passed on her information to Jake Roberts, our sales guy."

"Was that the extent of your involvement?"

Cassandra replied, "Yes, I never heard anything from Renee after the initial phone call. I just passed along her name and phone number to Jake telling him that the contact needed help with a stalker. I didn't talk to Renee after that, and neither Jake nor Jason provided me with any follow up information after I referred Renee. I had no idea whether Mindefusement took her on as a client or not."

"Thank you, Ms. Jenkins. You're dismissed." Zavoina replied.

The next witness called by Zavoina was Renee. After his preliminary questions as to her name, employment status, and education, he asked: "What is your relationship with Mindefusement and its owners or employees?"

Renee was emotional as a witness for a couple of reasons. Despite her differences with her father, he was her only surviving parent, and she could not bear thinking of having both her father and brother in prison. She also felt that her call to Cassandra set in motion the events that led directly to Marc's assault and indirectly caused his suicide. Biting back tears, Renee responded, "I have no relationship with Mindefusement other than a friend from high school who works there and my father, who is the CEO."

"Who is this friend from Mindefusement?" Zavoina asked.

Renee said, "Cassandra Jenkins."

"And why did you call on Ms. Jenkins?"

Renee, with downcast eyes and her lips trembling, replied, "Look, I was being stalked and had no idea how to stop it. I knew Cassandra had connections and might be able to help or at least put me in touch with someone who could. I didn't realize it would lead to Marc's de…"

"His suicide." the prosecutor Interrupted her sharply.

"I didn't know! I just wanted him to stop!"

"Well, you got what you wanted, didn't you Ms. Shiner?" the prosecutor asked rhetorically. The prosecutor continued, "Did you have contact with any other employees at Mindefusement?"

"I talked to a guy named Jake Roberts, who assured me the stalking would stop. He didn't tell me what he was going to do."

"Were you aware that Marc Brown was hospitalized because of Jake's actions?"

"No, I just realized that shortly after I talked to Jake, the stalking stopped for about a month. Then Marc was back hounding me through messages and on social media.

He seemed to be watching me wherever I went. I called Jake back to let him know the stalking had resumed and he said he would take care of it."

"And shortly after that call, the stalking stopped for good?"

Renee replied hesitantly, "Yes."

"How and when did you become aware of Marc Brown's suicide after your final phone call with Jake?"

She replied, "A friend of mine at the college who knew about the stalking told me that Marc had committed suicide a few days after he died."

"What was your reaction to hearing that Marc was dead and wouldn't be stalking you or anyone else any more?"

"I was relieved that I would never look over my shoulder to find him following me, but I was shocked and a bit sad that someone I knew was dead by his own hand.

"That's all I have for you. Thank you, Ms. Shiner."

The next witness called was Julie Biggs. After going through the formalities, the prosecutor started his questioning off with a bomb, "As a fellow lawyer, you had to know your Mindefusement colleagues were committing a crime with regards to Marc Brown."

"Jason Wilson held a secret meeting with George Shiner and several others regarding reputation destruction. I was not invited to this meeting. I happened to walk by the office to deliver a memo and asked what was going on. I was aghast at the proposed new 'product' and gave them my legal opinion in uncertain terms: the entire concept was highly illegal, and if the company went forward with it, I was resigning immediately."

"Were you aware of Jason Wilson's and Jake Robert's activities with Marc Brown?"

"I learned about it after the fact," Julie replied.

"How did you learn about it?"

"The day after Mr. Shiner was informed by Jason and Jake of Marc's beating followed by the hacking of his cell phone and the cell tower, I was summoned for a meeting in the CEO's office where he gave me a short version of what had happened. I did a quick search and found that Marc Brown had been fired from his job and committed suicide. Jason and Jake were summoned to the CEO's office."

"What happened then?" asked Zavoina.

Julie responded, "Jason and Jake filled in the details. I couldn't understand why those two were still employed by Mindefusement. I demanded they be summarily fired and and the appropriate legal authorities informed. The CEO, George Shiner, didn't see it my way. I advised him that if he didn't follow my advice, I would have no choice but to immediately resign and inform the authorities myself."

Zavoina asked, "But you didn't, did you?"

"No, I didn't because of circumstances involving my brother, Stuart. May I explain?"

"By all means." Zavoina replied.

"My younger brother, Stuart, had been charged with assault four years ago. Stuart is bipolar, and our parents had died in a head-on car accident which triggered a manic episode. In this manic state, he believed the husband of a coworker was abusing her. Stuart attacked security guards at the husband's workplace. An agreement was entered with the Assistant District Attorney for Stuart to be placed in a psychiatric facility," said Julie as tears welled up in her eyes from the memory. "May I have some water please, before I continue?"

Zavoina poured her a glass from his table and handed it to Julie. She took a sip followed by a deep breath and continued.

"My parents' estate was sued for wrongful death leaving us without funds to maintain Stuart in even a halfway decent facility. He was basically warehoused with junkies and criminals. He wasn't really receiving any kind of treatment and was wasting away doped up on meds."

Julie continued, "I was employed by a reputable law firm, but the cost of this third-rate mental health institute was the best I could afford since I was paying off the lawyers in defending the wrongful death action. And then, the firm fired me because seeing Stuart as often as possible and the stress of my parents' death and concerns for Stuart's well-being was affecting my performance."

Julie took another sip of water. "I was called into the executive partner's office, and informed that my brother's condition was a liability and was fired. I snapped when Mr. Hinkley referred to my brother as a liability and threw a chair at him. My reputation as a lawyer was in the toilet at that point. I couldn't find employment as a lawyer."

Zavoina asked, "So it was this point that George Shiner and Mindefusement came into the picture?"

"My résumé was posted on a number of online job

websites. I was contacted by Mindefusement to come in for an interview. I was reluctant to take the job as I had no information about Mindefusement or its practices. I shadowed a few calls to get me acquainted with the nature of the business, which was filming clients' fantasies in custom, tailor-made, videos. One of the perks offered if I accepted the appointment as general counsel was to pay for my brother's care at a first rate facility."

"So what happened when you threatened to resign?" Zavoina asked.

"The CEO told me point blank my resignation would result in Stuart immediately being evicted from the mental health facility since that was a part of the terms of my employment. He further stated that I would be even less employable than I was after my prior termination," Julie replied choking back sobs.

"Ms. Biggs, why did you not resign?"

The usual self-confident Julie stammered in response: "W-while I couldn't care less wh-what h-happened to m-m-me, I c-couldn't let m-my brother suffer."

"So then what happened?" Zavoina asked.

Julie dabbed at her eyes with a tissue, took a sip of water and several deep breaths before responding: "The CEO refused to fire Jason and Jake over their actions. He took care of the problems with accounting, and pursued a cover-up of Jason's and Jake's involvement with Marc Brown's assault and hacking in New York."

"Ms. Biggs, as an officer of the court, you knew such a cover-up was illegal, and by not coming forward with the information, you would be considered a principal in the cover-up and an accomplice after the fact."

"Knowing that Renee was the CEO's daughter, I could understand his desire to protect her just as I needed to protect my brother, so to a certain extent I let that interfere with my judgment."

"We've covered a lot of ground." Zavoina said. He then asked, "Ms. Biggs, have you been offered a plea deal in exchange for your testimony?"

"No, I have not." she replied.

"And yet you have provided testimony to the grand jury incriminating yourself when you could have taken the Fifth Amendment and refused to answer. Why?"

"George Shiner's emotional blackmail was wrong, but lying under oath or taking the Fifth goes against everything I believe in as an attorney."

The prosecutor let Julie's response sink in for a few moments, and then said, "Thank you, Ms. Biggs. You are dismissed."

Zavoina's next witness was Jake Roberts. After the preliminary questions, he asked, "What was your position at Mindefusement?"

Jake replied, "I worked as their sales guy. I interfaced with clients who wanted to make fantasy videos. I did most of the pre-screening to make sure we had viable clients."

"I'm not familiar with the term pre-screening other than with regard to credit card offers. Could you please elaborate on what you mean by 'pre-screening?'"

"Pre-screening is simply getting on a call with the potential client and determining if he or she is a good candidate for filming their fantasy. We make sure the potential clients understand that they are not getting a real-life version of their fantasy. If a client does not pass pre-screening, we simply refund the deposit and move on to the next potential client."

"Thank you," Zavoina replied. He then asked, "How did you get involved with Marc Brown?"

Jake hesitated and drank some water before replying, "I received a lead from Cassandra Jenkins regarding a stalking situation for Renee Shiner. I then passed that information to Jason Wilson. We discussed the situation, and since Mindefusement didn't have a product that would work in this instance, we determined that possibly threatening Marc might work. We agreed to hire some muscle to have a talk with him, but only a talk. Never did we intend any physical harm come to Marc."

"Who else knew about your hiring persons to intimidate Marc Brown?" Zavoina asked.

"Just me and Jason at that point," Jake responded. "Both of us were shocked when the bouncers went way beyond our instructions, but we thought that was the end of Renee's problem."

The prosecutor quickly followed up: "But it wasn't, was it, Mr. Roberts?"

Jake took another drink of water and continued, "A few weeks later, Renee called me back. She was frantic because the stalking had started again and was even worse than before. Jason and I discussed the matter and decided that this was a perfect opportunity to prove the effectiveness of reputation destruction as a new service to offer Mindefusement clients who wanted more than just a fantasy video. Jason Wilson set up the hack of Marc Brown's phone to send out a message that he was a stalker."

"And what was the result of hacking the cell tower and Marc's cell phone?"

"His reputation was immediately destroyed. The people in the store started scolding Marc. A video of the encounter with customers was posted to Facebook. Later, we learned he lost his job. And then, he committed suicide."

"Were you aware that hiring bouncers to intimidate Mr. Brown, even though they went beyond that and assaulted him, was illegal?" the prosecutor asked.

"Yes," Jake replied.

"Were you aware that hacking his cell phone was illegal?"

"Yes, we were informed that it was totally illegal by Ms. Biggs when it was brought up during our initial meeting regarding reputation destruction."

"So why did you do it?!" Zavoina asked angrily.

"The CEO of Mindefusement, George Shiner, expressed that he was open to the idea of reputation destruction under the right circumstances. Since his daughter was the stalker's victim, Jason and I decided to use it against Marc Brown."

"When did Mr. Shiner find out about your actions against Mr. Brown?" Zavoina asked.

"When accounting informed Mr. Shiner about the expense reports Jason turned in for his actions in New York. It was at that point I was called into the CEO's office, informed him regarding hiring the bouncers, the assault and hospitalization, the continued stalking, and the use of reputation destruction by hacking Marc's cell phone."

"And what was Mr. Shiner's reaction when you informed him of your and Jason's actions?"

Jake replied, "He was livid at first. Then when he found out the victim was his daughter, he softened his stance and decided it was better to pursue a cover-up with accounting and legal."

"What was Julie Biggs' reaction?" Zavoina asked.

"She told Mr. Shiner to fire us immediately and turn us over to the authorities. When the CEO refused, she threatened to resign."

"Did Mr. Shiner attempt to blackmail Ms. Biggs to be complicit in the cover-up?"

"Yes, he used her brother's continued psychiatric treatment at a good facility against her as well as threatened that she would never work as a lawyer again." Jake replied.

Zavoina thanked Jake for his testimony and dismissed him.

The grand jury heard the rest of the witnesses and testimony and the indictments Assistant U.S. Attorney Zavoina wanted against those persons involved with Mindefusement. Their deliberation was brief, and the indictments were quickly returned.

Jake and Jason were indicted under the Truth in Caller ID Act of 2009 for hacking Marc Brown's cell phone as was Michael Lee, the technician who orchestrated the hack. Jake and Jason also faced state charges for the intimidation and assault of Marc Brown along with the bouncers.

George Shiner was indicted as a conspirator after the fact for violating the Truth in Caller ID Act of 2009. Julie was indicted on the same charge.

George Shiner, Julie Biggs, Jake Roberts, Jason Wilson, and Michael Lee were arraigned in federal court a few days after the indictments were handed down by the grand jury.

George Shiner's arraignment was held before a U.S. Magistrate, the Honorable Richard Briccetti at the Daniel Patrick Moynihan United States Courthouse. The CEO appeared along with the senior partner, Jackson Murdock, and two associates from a boutique New York City law firm whose area of practice was criminal law. The defense attorney waived the reading of the indictment.

The judge asked: "What is your client's plea to the indictments?"

"Not guilty, your honor," the CEO responded confidently as instructed by his counsel.

"Recommendations for bail, Mr. Zavoina?" asked the judge.

"We request bail in the amount of $500,000, that the defendant surrender his passport, and be subject to house arrest in order to return to Texas pending trial," Zavoina replied.

Murdock responded, "Your honor, Mr. Shiner has no prior convictions, is a model citizen, and is not a flight risk. We request that he be released on his own recognizance. We agree to the surrender of his passport, but he has responsibilities he must perform at Mindefusement, and we do not agree to house arrest."

Briccetti took a few moments to mull over the arguments and said: "I will set bail at $100,000, have the defendant turn over his passport, and agree to house arrest. In this day and age, he can take care of his business from his home."

George Shiner wasn't happy with the judge's decision, but Murdock had prepared him, and he immediately posted bail. He reported to the U.S. Marshal's office and was fitted with an ankle bracelet. One of the U.S. Marshals would escort him to his flight back to Dallas where another U.S. Marshal from Dallas would take him to his home.

A swarm of reporters were waiting outside the courthouse to question the CEO. There were also several dozen protestors held back by New York City Police. Mr. Shiner emerged from the courthouse with the U.S. Marshal as well as the CEO's personal bodyguard. Mr. Shiner was at the center of the Mindefusement scandal and had become a household name and a controversial figure.

William "Memphis" Brown patiently waited outside the courthouse in the throng of Mindefusement protestors. In Memphis' mind, the CEO was the embodiment of Mindefusement, the organization that had killed his younger brother. It and its leader needed to be destroyed. He didn't trust the justice system. It had not properly investigated Marc's death. Memphis knew that even if the CEO was convicted, all that would happen to him was being locked away in a cushy, federal prison. This wasn't satisfactory punishment for Marc Brown's suicide.

Memphis had purchased a handgun and spent hours in target practice. He was ready to inflict his carnage and take out the CEO. He wasn't intimidated by the police or the size of the crowd. Memphis viewed the CEO who had control and power over his employees at Mindefusement as the person responsible for his brother's death. George Shiner's family needed to suffer the same agony he suffered when Marc took his own life as the result of Mindefusement's actions.

A horde of reporters surrounded Mr. Shiner to question him as Memphis prepared to unleash his revenge. Mr. Shiner was the first to notice Memphis. He was with the protestors, but he stood out for some reason. Maybe it was the murderous rage in his eyes. Maybe because of the familial resemblance to Marc Brown whose picture in the funeral home obituary Shiner had seen. Then he saw it: a small pistol being drawn from Memphis' pocket. Memphis moved away from the protestors and drew closer to the CEO, breaking through the circle of reporters surrounding him.

The CEO panicked but was unsure of who to alert. Instinctively he called out, "Seize that man!" pointing at the man with the gun. But it was too late.

The CEO held up his left hand in defense, but the bullet tore through his hand and entered his chest. The second bullet entered his chest while the third shot hit him in the gut. Mr. Shiner hit the ground with his bodyguard and the U.S. Marshall protecting him from any subsequent shots.

Memphis was tackled by the police before he could

get off any additional shots. He screamed, "Rot in hell, you motherfucker!"

In his last moments, George Shiner looked toward the sky and saw the magnificent courthouse while those around him examined his wounds. He thought about his son, Richard, and his daughter, Renee, and hoped they would remember him fondly and forgive him for the attention he had paid to his businesses rather than his family.

The protestors had dispersed in a panic. The intrepid reporters had not. They had remained to film the shooting and its aftermath. George Shiner convulsed before closing his eyes for the last time.

EPILOGUE

Memphis Brown was charged with 1st-degree murder in the shooting death of George Shiner. He pled guilty and received a life sentence without the possibility for parole. He is currently serving his time in Attica. His celebrity, or rather his notoriety in outing Mindefusement and its involvement with the suicide of his brother, earned him the attention of a publisher who was interested in publishing an account of how Memphis managed to piece together what happened. Memphis is working with a ghostwriter on the book.

The two bouncers were charged with aggravated assault and both pled guilty. They each received ten years in a New York state prison and fines of $5,000.

Jason Wilson and Jake Roberts both pled guilty to federal charges and received five-year probationary sentences for their cooperation as well as hefty fines. They were also charged by the State of New York as accomplices to Marc Brown's aggravated assault. They are serving three years in a New York state prison on those charges.

The technician, Michael Lee, who orchestrated the hack of Marc's phone, pled guilty to his charges and received a plea deal for his cooperation. He was sentenced to five years in federal prison and a fine of $50,000.

Julie Biggs was offered a plea deal after her testimony before the grand jury and corroborating testimony regarding George Shiner's blackmail and coercion. She received two years probation. She was disbarred from the practice of law by the Texas Bar Association and moved to Edmond, Oklahoma. She freelances as a legal assistant to attorneys doing research and other clerical work while she waits to apply for reinstatement after five years.

Stuart Biggs' bipolar condition stabilized on appropriate medications. He was released from in-patient psychiatric care and moved in with his sister in Edmond. He found a job doing graphic design work and is currently under the care of a well-known Edmond psychiatrist. The psychiatrist sees him frequently to make any adjustments needed with his medication to avoid episodes of mania or depression, a balancing act faced by those with bipolar disorder.

Ben Hammond, head of accounting at Mindefusement, took over as CEO. He fired most of the staff that weren't subject to criminal charges including Cassandra and Amanda. He kept everyone in the film division. After a class action suit against the company was filed,

Mindefusement filed for bankruptcy protection, and all remaining assets of the company were liquidated.

Renee Shiner married Mario. She inherited George Shiner's estate. She settled several civil lawsuits against Mr. Shiner's estate and decided to change her name to Alexa Edwards. She and Mario moved to Los Angeles where Alexa pursued a career in acting.

ACKNOWLEDGEMENTS

I'd first like to thank my family for making this book possible. Without their support, this book would not have been finished.

I'd like to thank Bobby Sue Sargent for reading the first few draft concepts and encouraging me to see this book through.

I'd like to thank Dan Bruce and Wendy Belles for helping initially edit the book and providing ideas for the torture templates.

I'd especially like to Pauli Loeffler. She wasn't sold on the book at first but began to see the potential and helped shape the ending. She also edited the book on her own time to make Mindefusement a very entertaining novella.

I'd like to thank Chanel Lyon for proofreading this book.

I'd like to thank Kate Burgener for designing the book cover, spine, back cover, and placement of the text.

Finally, I'd like to thank the fans that have supported the book through Twitter and Facebook. Sorry for all my pesky emails and posts.

Thanks so much!
Ronald Huereca
Author of Mindefusement